Broken Hearts
and
Sticky Tape

PETER T. BISSETT

DEDICATION

This book is dedicated to the children of Ukraine affected by war, through no fault of their own.

The proceeds from the book are being donated to:

Ukraine Charity

https://www.ukrainecharity.org/

CONTENTS

ACKNOWLEDGMENTS

I would like to thank Natalie Parry for her help and advice on all things Ukrainian., and Madison King and Pauline Bissett for their ongoing support and encouragement.

TRAPPED
Inspired by: IMAGINE.
Performed by JOHN LENNON

My name is Iryna Kravchenko. That's a good start, I suppose. If I'm going to write all of my thoughts and fears here on this, my cellar wall, people will need to know who I am, who I was. My hand trembles, and tears begin to run down my face. Those three last little words, who I was, have suddenly hit home. I'm entombed down here, imprisoned for my sins. This is all I can do for myself, write and pray. Pray that when this is over, someone will read my story and hopefully understand the torment and agony that I have been going through.

The vast array of pencils and crayons I am using belonged to my daughter Olena. She will not be needing them now. Her body is somewhere above me, buried in the rubble that was once our home, our little farm. Like most six-year-olds, she was always drawing whatever came out of her tiny head, unicorns, and fairies with gossamer wings. Rainbows arced across the paper from one corner to the other. She was always so happy, always smiling.

Her smiling face still haunts me. It always will.

For however long I have left down here, I will see her young smiling face. The inquisitive looks when I was cooking, the constant questions. What herb was I putting in the stew? Why was I using so much salt? She was so full of questions, bright ideas, and a huge vibrant imagination.

I never understood where she got it all from. Not from me, and certainly not Pavlo, my husband. We are simple farmers. I've never even been to the nearest big city of Mariupol. In fact, at twenty-five years of age, I've been no further than the next village.

Outside, in that awful big wide world that we are now living in. Our tiny village, a few I know kilometres down the hillside, no longer exists. It hadn't done for several days before I became trapped down here. It had already been well and truly flattened, laid to waste by days of constant Russian shelling and bombardment. Then, without warning, our little farm seemed to be their next target. Olena had walked up to the milking shed with me. I was not particularly eager to leave her alone down at the farm anymore. She was singing quietly, affectionately rubbing the cow's muzzle when the first explosion came.

Her sweet, lyrical voice became a terrifying scream as a second blast rocked the building. The roof partially collapsed, sending splintering wooden beams and tiles raining down on us. I grabbed her hand, and we ran for the shelter of the house. We practiced this a few times when the village was being destroyed, never thinking we would actually be doing it for real one day.

We were heading for where I am now, our

small vegetable cellar. Pavlo had insisted that we put several spare oil lamps, plus an assortment of tinned food, down here. There is even running water, plus an old metal sink which we used to clean the turnips, beet, and potatoes.

I had just opened the door to the cellar when the third explosion came. It must have been a direct hit on the farmhouse. The whole house shook. Seconds later, the downstairs walls were blown out in all directions. Everything above us came crashing down. Walls, bedroom floorboards, bedroom furniture, the chimney stack. Everything.

Olena had just stepped away from me. She had cried that she needed her doll, the one I had made for her fourth birthday. It was never very far from her, but today, she had left it on the kitchen table rather than carrying it up to the milking shed for whatever reason.

Wanting her doll had killed her. I had killed her as well. I had ended her young life by not keeping her safe by my side. Letting go of her tiny hand and allowing her to go and get her doll. I had killed my daughter. I was concentrating too much on trying to open the old cellar door.

Before the devastating blast sent me tumbling headlong down the stone cellar stairs, my last image of Olena was seeing no more than her pale dusty hand protruding from beneath a mountain of bricks and rubble, still clutching her rag doll. That image will remain with me for the rest of my life, however long that may be. My little girl is gone, and all because of me. More tears begin to sting my eyes and roll down my cheeks.

I looked at my name scribbled on the cellar

wall, and even seeing that made me cry more salty tears. I needed to be stronger than this. While I'm still breathing, I'm still living. Those selfish thoughts prick my conscience and stab at my heart. Especially with Olena's favourite purple crayon still warm in my hand.

My name is Iryna Kravchenko. This little vegetable cellar is all that remains of our farmhouse. 01-06-22. Day One. What in God's name is going on in this world? How can another country think they have the right just to come and take our land from us? Are they so stupid that they think we would roll over and allow that to happen to us?

Tears were flowing freely again. I wiped the back of my hand across my face. I was cross and angry. My rant over. I went back to the wall.

What is going to happen to me? Will someone come? I fear not. Everything above me has gone. There will be nothing for anyone to see except perhaps for my daughter, Olena. I pray that by some miracle, someone will find her body and do the right thing by her.

I stepped away from the wall. The thought of my daughter lying up there was really upsetting. What was the point of doing all this? No one is coming to save me, except perhaps the Russians, and they certainly won't be very friendly towards me. The thought of them finding me down here made me shiver.

My guilt has now taken over. It has slowly been gnawing away at me from the inside, eating away at my soul and getting the better of me. My heart feels sorry for itself as if it could stop at any moment, and my life would end.

I tossed Olena's crayon to one side. I needed a distraction, a big one. I summoned up the energy and checked the cellar door above me. I crawled up the cold steps on my hands and knees, every muscle in my body aching. The door was lying flat against the opening. There was a slight gap in one corner. I could smell the air outside but couldn't tell if it was day or night. So much more rubble must have fallen. I tried pushing at the door, but nothing happened. It didn't move. I guess my theory is correct, that the remains of our house are now piled on top of it, making it impossible for me to lift it.

Day Two.02-06-2022. I cannot remember what happened to me yesterday. I woke and found myself in the far corner of the cellar. My body was stiff all over with pain. I was cold and shaking, thirsty and hungry. I have no recollection of how I managed to get there. The last thing I remember doing was being at the top of the cellar steps crying.

Standing and looking around the cellar properly for the first time, I took stock. I needed to be in control. If this were to be my prison, I would run it the way I wanted to. I knew very little. What I did know, however, was that it was now light outside. There is one tiny window down here situated at the highest point, where the wall meets the ceiling. Although it seems almost completely blocked with earth and other rubble, I can see a little chink of the sky. From now on, the little window will be my clock.

I have now organised myself in between my

crying and my guilt. I have now positioned three oil lamps. One at the top of the cellar steps. One by where I shall try and sleep, and the last one, which is alight now, on the old wooden table where we prepared the vegetables when our lives were normal.

The water supply is still on. I found nine empty, rather dusty wine bottles beneath a very smelly, thick piece of plastic. I suspect Pavlo has secretly been drinking down here. I would forgive him in a heartbeat if he were to return home and find me. Why he ever took the hunting rifle and left us makes no sense. It didn't then, and it doesn't now.

I suppose he felt compelled to go by the others. Four turned up in a rusty old white pickup and said they knew a few Russian soldiers had been cut off from the main group and were hiding in the woods a few kilometres from here. He couldn't look me in the eye when he climbed into the back of the truck. Olena had pulled at his hand and begged. He didn't answer her plea to stay or kiss either of us goodbye.

I have filled those empty wine bottles and the metal sink to the brim with water, just in case the supply suddenly ceases without warning. My first drink of water wasn't a pleasant experience. It was warm on my lips and throat. It had a strange earthy aftertaste, but it's all I have, and it was palatable, but only just.

Day Three. 03-06-2022. I didn't sleep well last night, and there was so much noise from the shelling and loud explosions. I cannot imagine who is being bombarded so intensely, although Mariupol is, of course, less than twenty kilometres from here. Being a city and an important port,

perhaps that is the target. My prayers are with them.
I haven't achieved very much so far today. Severe stomach pain
has restricted my movement. Probably the water. I can hardly
stand up at the moment. I need to rest once more.

I looked back at the wall. My writing beneath the day three heading was scratchy, and even I struggled to read what I had written. My vision seems impaired, and my eyes have begun to water. I fall to my knees. I must crawl across the concrete floor to get to my makeshift bed. A few old woven sacks that we stored the vegetables in.

Having collapsed on the sacking, I have suddenly become boiling, and my face is dripping with sweat. My arms are damp and clammy but feel cold to the touch of my fingers. A sharp, intense pain rips through my stomach. My knees automatically bend towards my head as I curl up into the foetal position. Screams of abdominal pain echo through the once silent cellar. I try and clamp my lips together, but without success. The pain is too unbearable.

Tears are now rolling down my cheeks. My hands are in fists as I pound them, one after the other, on the floor. Another wave of pain ripples through my body. I roll over and punch the wall in desperation. It does nothing to relieve the agony going on inside my body. I don't know what to do. I'm trapped, a prisoner in my own cellar. I've been entombed alive. My mind isn't clear. It's wandering all over the place. Then, there was nothing.

Looking up and squinting through bleary eyes. The little window, my clock, tells me it is daytime outside, but nothing more than that. I raise myself up on one elbow and realise that the pain has eased slightly. I manage to stagger across to the wall and write.

Day Four. 04-06-2022. I haven't eaten anything yet. My stomach feels as though someone has tried to drive a sharp stick through my stomach from the inside. It's tender to my touch. I also know that it would reject any food that I offered. The loneliness, too, is unbearable.

The back of my throat is desperate for water. I have sipped a little, but I haven't swallowed any. I couldn't bear to go through a night like that again. My head has started spinning now, and I need to lie back down. Scribbling on the wall felt like a mammoth task, and it has drained my energy completely. I can hardly stand now. My legs have turned to jelly.

I staggered drunkenly across the floor to the rough sacks and collapsed on top of them. I suddenly realized that the shelling had stopped. The constant noise was frightening, but this felt worse. Sitting here now is so eerie. It's as though the world has ceased. Has everyone gone away? I cannot imagine that they have. This silence is troubling me more than the explosions. It has also made me realise just how alone I really am.

Pavlo said two days. He promised he would stay safe and return in two days. According to the wall, I have been down here for four. And they have been four of the most unbearable days of my life.

From out of nowhere, Olena jumped into my thoughts. If I felt sad or overtired, she would come and offer me her rag doll. We would sit, and I would bounce her doll gently on my lap, talking to it, pretending we were having a conversation. Sometimes we just needed a moment. Mother and daughter time, together, bonding. She would smile and always say the same words to me. "It will be alright, Mama. Papa will be home soon. He will hug us both, and we will be fine."

She was right, of course. Pavlo always came home, often exhausted and tired, but he always managed a smile and the big hug she constantly talked about. Now, there was nothing, no home, no Olena. His little girl, who he idolised, has gone. His farm, which he worked so hard to keep running, has also gone. There is nothing left for either of us.

My thoughts of them both start me crying again. If he suddenly appeared, what would I say to him? How will I ever be able to look him in the eyes, knowing it was my fault that our child is no longer with us? I closed my eyes and listened to nothing. My head was swimming in a sea of silence. My mind drifted towards the distant, tiny island of contentment.

"Iryna. Iryna." A muffled voice called my name. I jumped from my makeshift bed. "Yes, I'm here." I stood looking around the cellar. My eyes desperately tried to focus around the room. There was no one here. My life hadn't suddenly changed. I was still all alone. I had dreamt the whole thing.

Sudden movement above my head near the top of the cellar steps made me jump. I clasped one hand to my mouth, the other to my pounding heart. People were working up there, moving bricks and other rubble. I could hear all the pounding and crashing as someone threw things aside.

I had new life inside my body. Excitedly I rushed to the bottom of the cellar steps and stared upwards. The old dirty white door across the opening was bending as heavy boots were trampling over it. I heard someone grunt loudly as something hefty was dragged away from it. I couldn't control myself any longer.

"I'm here. I'm down here." I screamed at the top of my voice. "Iryna. I'm coming." It was Pavlo. He had returned. Tears flowed down my cheeks. Only this time, they were tears of joy.

"Two more minutes Iryna. Just two more minutes." He banged twice on the cellar door as if to make the point. My heart was thumping. I knew there were going to be tears of happiness and tears of sorrow when we spoke. But I loved him so much that I knew we would get through this. Broken hearts have a way of healing. We would start again together.

I held my breath as somebody finally lifted the old door. It was Pavlo himself. He stood there, holding it up like a flimsy piece of white cardboard, before tossing it aside. Fresh air rushed down into the cellar. I took several welcoming breaths of cool air before walking up the first two concrete steps. Then I opened my arms with a broad smile on my face.

The sound of a weapon going off reached me before Pavlo's crumpled body did. I screamed and grappled with his tumbling torso before cradling him in my arms. Blood slowly trickled from a corner of his mouth.

"The Russians promised they wouldn't hurt us. They said they wanted an end to this madness." I shushed him. I told him not to speak, but he carried on. "They just wanted food and fresh water. I even joked with one of them about him taking a bath here." He coughed, and more blood escaped and ran down his wiry black beard.

"It's okay, Pavlo. It's okay." I lied to him, probably for the first and last time ever.

"I got detached from the other guys on the first night and headed back to you and Olena." I watched his pained face as he thought about her. "Where is she? Where is our daughter?" The question I was dreading most had just passed his lips. Yet, my answer was so easy. I raised my eyes and looked up. I could now see the sky clearly for the first time in days. "She's waiting up there for you," I replied. I had no idea if he understood what I meant, but he raised an eyebrow and managed a half smile. Then he slowly closed his eyes and slipped away. He was gone.

I had no tears. My husband's worst nightmare was over. Mine was probably just about to begin, especially when I saw one of the six Russian soldiers grinning down at me, with Olena's ragdoll sticking out of the top of his dirty filthy tunic.

INNOCENT LOVE

Inspired by: BILLIE JEAN.
Performed by MICHAEL JACKSON

The two seventeen-year-olds sat nervously in the solicitor's office, with both sets of parents in attendance. Sarah Jane and Scott both had their heads bowed. They both knew the trouble they were in. Everything had escalated, but it wasn't all down to the youngsters. Sarah Jane scratched at a bit of old nail polish on her thumb while Scott stared down at the multi-coloured patterned carpet. They were both waiting nervously. They both knew that all hell was going to be let loose.

Someone had purposely positioned the chairs both families were sitting on to create a defining line between the two bitter families. They were all facing the large dark brown desk of the middle-aged solicitor, whose name neither youngster could remember. His name seemed to be the least of their worries.

The two families were here because Sarah Jane Milton was having a baby and claiming that Scott Andrews was the father. Her parents didn't find out until Sarah Jane could no longer hide the bump. Although her mother had her suspicions, she hadn't asked any questions and certainly hadn't mentioned it to her husband. His quick-fire temper would have erupted into an all-out war, which is precisely how it felt at this moment.

For their part, Mr and Mrs Andrews were both adamant that their son wasn't that type of boy. At seventeen, he was still attending High School, studying hard. Girls were the last thing on his mind. Sarah Jane's parents believe their only daughter, she says it was Scott that made her pregnant, and they are demanding the truth and justice for her.

Before they arrived here at the point of no return, neither parent had listened correctly to what the youngsters had to say. They had hardly got a word in. Every time one of them had something to say or tried to explain, one of the parents, usually the father, told them they would deal with it. They would sort it all out.

The solicitor had seen this all before. He had even written a paper on dealing with angry parents in young paternity cases. It was well received and was often used and quoted by some of the young up-and-coming solicitors throughout the country.

"Right then. First things first. Let me introduce myself. I'm David Simpson. I have called this early meeting to see if we can find an answer without it all spiralling out of control. I want this meeting to be as amicable as possible, please. I realise there is a lot of tension within the room, but we will get nowhere, being uncivilised towards each other." He hadn't meant to look at Mr Milton, but his eyes automatically drifted in that direction.

It had been Sarah Jane's father that had bombarded his office with phone calls, trying to get the meeting brought forward. *"I'm baying for blood."* He had shouted down the phone once when he didn't hear the correct answers.

"Sarah Jane. In your own words, I would like to hear your account of the night in question." He sat back in his chair and steepled his hands together.

Sarah Jane placed her hands beneath her now expanded stomach and took a deep breath.

"We had gone to Benjamin's eighteenth birthday party." David Simpson held up his hand.

"When you say we? You mean you and Scott?"

Sarah Jane nodded, and her eyes flashed across to her parents.

"You never mentioned that you went with him." Her father emphasised the last word. Sarah Jane didn't reply. She just sat there looking awkward.

"Please carry on, Sarah Jane." The solicitor asked, breaking the uncomfortable silence.

"There were a lot of older teenagers there. Some, I guess in their early twenties. There was a lot of drink about, beer, vodka, red and white wine, that sort of thing. When we arrived, some seemed drunk already. I think that there were drugs there too. But I was never offered any." She quickly added before her father could jump in and embarrass her even more.

"Benjamin said that his parents wouldn't be back until midnight. And for us to enjoy his party. I don't think I saw him again. They live in a massive five-bedroomed house." She closed her eyes as soon as she mentioned the word bedroom.

"I bet you knew all about that, Scott?" Her father remarked sarcastically as he leant forward and looked across the room.

"Mr Milton, please!" David Simpson said firmly. "Allow your daughter to finish." Sarah Jane's father sat back and folded his arms. Glaring at the solicitor as he did so.

"Scott got us both a vodka and lemonade. I commented that mine was rather strong. He tasted it, went over to where the drinks were and topped it with more lemonade." Everyone in the room heard Mr Milton say, *"yeah, right."*

"We danced for a bit, had a few more vodkas, and then Scott suggested we went upstairs."

"I need to ask you, Sarah Jane. Were you already in a relationship with Scott?"

"Don't be bloody stupid. Of course, she wasn't."

"Yes." Sarah Jane's voice was no more than a whisper, but it answered her father's remark.

In an instant, he was on his feet and stepping across the invisible dividing line that separated both families. Scott's father was just as nimble and quick to react. He stood and blocked Mr Milton.

"Mr Andrews. Mr Milton. Please, this is getting us nowhere. Please sit back down. Both men stood their ground, eye ball to eye ball. One was smiling, the other scowling. Eventually, Mr Milton went back to his seat. His wife rested her hand on his arm, which he immediately brushed away.

"Carry on, Sarah Jane." David Simpson said once the fidgeting had stopped and everyone seemed settled.

"We went upstairs." She stopped and looked at her mother. Mrs Milton offered her daughter her hand, which she accepted gratefully. The warm squeeze of tender fingers gave her the confidence to continue. "We walked into one of the bedrooms. It looked as if someone else had been there before us, but it was dark, and neither of us turned the lights on. I lay on the bed and waited for Scott to join me. And we made love." She gripped her mother's hand even tighter, expecting her father to explode, but nothing happened. It was as if he had now switched off. As if he was no longer interested. She thought that perhaps he had now disowned her or something, just as bizarre.

"Thank you, Sarah Jane." David Simpson looked across to Scott. "Is that how you remember the evening panning out, Scott?" he asked again, steepling his hands in his familiar way.

"Well, we certainly had a few vodkas and lemonade, but I couldn't tell you how many. And I certainly asked Sa Ja."

"It's Sarah Jane. My daughter's name is Sarah Jane."

"Mr Milton, please."

Scott nodded and continued. "I certainly asked Sarah Jane if she wanted to go upstairs, but as soon as she flopped on the bed, I realised that she had passed out. I panicked. I checked that she was breathing, then I hurried down the stairs, straight out the front door, and ran down to the park. Benjamin lives at the end of the road, and their house backs onto the park. I went and sat on one of the swings and tried to work out what I should do next." Scott stopped and looked at Sarah Jane as if he expected her to agree with him. All he saw was her father shaking his head furiously.

"When you're ready, Scott." David Simpson wanted to keep the momentum going.

"I was probably sat on the swing for about twenty minutes, perhaps a little longer. When my phone suddenly pinged. I knew it was Sarah Jane. We both have the same funny ringtone. It's the sound of a toilet flushing." Sarah's mother gripped her daughter's hand tight, and her eyes widened. Now she understood. She had heard that sound from her daughter's phone so often recently and hadn't realised who it was. David Simpson also knew the sound and allowed himself a wry smile. He and his wife used the same ringtone to send each other messages.

"And what did the message say, Scott?" He asked, trying to keep his face straight while conducting this very tense meeting.

"It said. *Where are you?*" I immediately told her I was down at the park and heading back straight away. Sarah Jane met me at the front door. She said that she was feeling ill and wanted to go home. We didn't even go back in the house to say goodbye."

"And you walked her straight home from Benjamin's?"

"Yes, sir. She was rather unsteady on her feet and complained about feeling sick. But I put my arm around her, and we staggered home. It was still quite early, her parent's car wasn't on the drive, and she said they were also out for the evening. So, I kissed her, hugged her, and as far as I know, she went straight to bed."

"You didn't go inside the house?"

"No, sir. We hadn't spoken at all on the way home. As I said, Sarah Jane was a bit unbalanced. I thought it was best to leave her once I knew she was in safely."

David Simpson looked across at Sarah Jane.

Tears were running down her face. It was as if she had never heard this tale of events before, but Scott knew she had. They had talked about it in secret on several occasions.

She wiped away the tears, and everyone heard her sniffles. Her mother removed a paper tissue from her handbag and gave it to her daughter. With the help of her mother's assuring words, Sarah Jane composed herself and took a deep breath.

"Sarah Jane, how does that bode with you?" David Simpson asked. "Is there some truth in what Scott has just said?" She was already nodding. Her father glanced in her direction and stood up.

"Oh no. Scott is just putting ideas in her head. He has taken advantage of my daughter and is now trying to wriggle out of his responsibilities." All through his little rage, he was finger-pointing at Scott.

"Please sit down, Mr Milton." David Simpson asked, sounding exasperated by all of his stupid interruptions.

Eventually, he did as he was told, but not before muttering a few more obscenities under his breath and sitting with his arms folded across his chest.

"Scott helped me home, and he kissed and hugged me." Her voice trailed off. She didn't want to ask the one question that was bouncing around inside her head. She was too frightened of the answer. The very thought of it made her cry even more.

"Shall we take a ten-minute break?" David Simpson suggested, standing and walking towards the door before anyone could object. He opened it and spoke with the receptionist. "Margaret, be an angel and escort Mr and Mrs Milton and Sarah Jane to the back office, and I'll take Mr and Mrs Andrews and Scott to the interview room.

"Oh, so you can speak with them privately. Give them a few pointers." Mr Milton was shouting as he followed David out of the door.

"Margaret, change of plan. Take the Andrews family through to the back office. I'll deal with Mr and Mrs Milton and Sarah Jane. Would you be so kind as to follow me, please?" As David asked the question, he turned away and walked across the hall, unable to control the smile on his face. *"That went to plan then."* He said to himself, opening the office door.

He offered all three seats and perched himself on the corner of the large desk. "Mr Milton, you are doing yourself no favours with these outbursts." He spoke quietly. His voice had a kind ring to it.

"Henry is very overprotective of Sarah Jane. She is our only child. To us, she will always be our little girl." Mrs Milton said, smiling at her daughter.

"Our little girl has been made pregnant by him up the hall. Who has taken advantage of her, seducing her while she was unconscious. I want the little brat strung up by his. You know what." Henry Milton's angry, evil tongue was back.

"Look, I know this has been mentioned before, but a DNA test by both parties would clear all this up instantly." David Simpson looked at both parents, and only one of them looked happy.

"Sarah Jane is the one to ask. She has a phobia regarding needles." Mrs Milton spoke first, but Henry Milton wasn't very far behind.

"Why should Sarah Jane go through that? She has been humiliated and degraded enough, just having to sit through all this." For once, Sarah Jane was on her father's side. She couldn't stand the sight of hypodermic needles. They terrified her to the point that she ran away from school twice when she was younger. Even so, she nodded when David Simpson looked at her for an answer.

"Right then, let's pursue that line of attack. I'll get Margaret to bring in some tea and biscuits, and we'll convene again at four thirty." He stood up and walked out of the office.

Margaret Gilmore was probably the best receptionist that Wardle and Simpson had ever employed. At fifty-five, she was very savvy and loyal. She had always worked in the profession with some of the top lawyers in the country. Wardle and Simpson were fortunate to have her.

As David Simpson stepped out of the office, she walked towards him, carrying a tray of tea with an assortment of different biscuits. There was even a glass of cordial for Sarh Jane.

"The Andrews family have had theirs. I thought that perhaps you needed a little bit longer, with you know who?" She smiled, and David gave her a peck on the cheek.

"No. That's not going to happen. My son is not going to do a DNA test. Not for you or anyone else."

"Mr Andrews, if Scott says he didn't sleep with Sarah Jane, then he has nothing to worry about." David Simpson was trying to stay calm.

"He has nothing to worry about anyway. He has given us his word that he has not slept with her, and that's good enough for us." David Simpson huffed slightly before trying a new tack.

"Mr Andrews. If you refuse, it will end up in court, and a judge will demand that you allow your son to take a DNA test. That will cost you money. It will cost both families money. Is it really worth it?"

"Scott is not the father. End of story."

"Then I don't think I can do anymore for either of you."

Mr Andrews stepped forward and shook his hand. "I guess we're going to court then."

David Simpson broke the news to Mr and Mrs Milton.

"He'll pay. The court will make him." Henry Milton was spitting feathers.

"Not necessarily, Mr Milton. You have to consider the DNA result.

The preliminary meeting was adjourned, with both parents still blaming each other. The meeting hadn't resolved anything. That night Scott texted Sarah Jane.

How are you holding up?

Okay, I guess. You?

Yea, bloody parents are a nightmare, though.

Tell me about it. Embarrassing or what?

My dad called you a spoilt little brat when we got home.

Charming.

I did defend you. I told him that he didn't know you.

Actually, my dad was a whole lot worse.

He wants you strung up by your unmentionables.

What!

Yep, until the weight of your suspended body rips itself free of them and you crash to the ground.

Weird lot, parents.

Just be careful, Scott. I'm going to be one soon.
Oh yes. Hey, about that.
Got to go. I'm about to get a visit. There's creaking on the
stairs.
Speak again soon.

Scott sat back on his bed and reflected on the day's events. He couldn't understand her parents. Where was all of this anger coming from? At least her mother acted relatively normal, but her father was like a hornless devil. He was evil. The words that came out of his mouth were toxic acid. Why didn't they believe him? That said, his father was just as bull-headed. It seemed to him that all four needed a kick up the backside. He smiled at his thoughts. The times he had heard his father say precisely the same words to him.

Sarah Jane strolled through the park. She was heavily pregnant, the baby had been kicking for several weeks now, and the birth was imminent. That said, Sarah Jane didn't seem to have a care in the world on this, her special day. The sky was blue, the June air was warm against her skin, and more importantly, she could see Scott waiting down by the little wooden bridge on the other side of the meadow.

They kissed without saying a word. Scott tenderly touched the bump that they had nicknamed Rolo.

"Happy eighteenth birthday Sarah Jane." Scott produced a small white box from behind his back and gave it to her.

She smiled, leaning forward and kissing his neck. The box contained a silver bracelet, with just one charm hanging from it, two hearts linked together.

"Why, thank you, kind sir." She said, putting the bracelet on her right wrist and inspecting it more closely. "It's lovely, Scott. Thank you."

"Yours next week." She said, watching him smile and nod.

"Hey, I've just realised I'm older than you."

"Four days, that's all."

"But four days is four days." She stepped away from him, still smiling. "What do you think is going to happen tomorrow, Scott?" She asked, sounding concerned.

"Well, I still believe you shouldn't have pushed it and agreed to a DNA test."

"Hold on, Scott Andrews, you agreed as well. In fact, you had to persuade your father to change his mind and allow you to take a controlled DNA test. It wasn't all down to me." Scott was already nodding, acknowledging the truth.

"Only because you wanted an end to all of this." Sarah Jane stepped forward and kissed him.

"I just wish I knew who the father was, Scott. It was so dark in that bloody bedroom when I woke up and saw who I thought was you. I didn't protest or anything. It was supposed to be our first time. Something to remember for the rest of our lives. And I'm sure my father won't rest until he finds out."

"No one is to blame, Sarah Jane. We will get through this. I promise. In a few days, we will both officially be adults. We can make our own choices."

Everyone was seated and waiting patiently. Scott looked across the tiny medical room, Sarah Jane caught his eye, and he half smiled. She saw him take out his phone. She felt her phone vibrate in her hand and saw the screen light up.

Will you marry me?

What!!!

I love you, Sarah Jane. Will you marry me?

Scott sat staring down at his screen. When no reply came, he felt dejected. Hesitantly he looked across at her. Her blue eyes were wide with excitement, and a warm smile covered her face. At that very moment, a nurse parted the blue plastic curtains and stepped out of a cubicle.

"Sarah Jane Milton?" She enquired, looking around the small waiting area. Sarah Jane rose to her feet. "Yes, I will, Scott Andrews." Her voice echoed through the silent room. Most people turned to look at her. Scott's parents chose to look at their son. He was beaming from one ear to the other and nodding happily.

The nurse glared at everyone sitting waiting. "Can we have a bit of hush, please? And will someone tell me what is going on?"

Scott stood up and took a deep breath. "I've just asked Sarah Jane to marry me, and she has accepted my proposal. So, whatever the rest of the world thinks of us. We don't much care." Sarah Jane shuffled across the room and took his hand, and together they walked into the waiting cubicle.

COSA NOSTRA

Inspired by: BOHEMIAN RHAPSODY.
Performed by QUEEN

I just wanted to be one of them, to be part of who they were. To be accepted into the Scorpions. No one in our little town of Borgetto has ever been good enough to have been given the honour of becoming a Scorpion. They are a gang who are just one step down from being full-fledged members of the Mafia. Mostly youngsters like me, aged from ten to twenty years old.

I had tried many times before to make contact, and now time is running out for me. I will be eighteen next May, and being a member of the Scorpions will change my life. I would always have money in my back pocket and much more acceptable clothes than these hand-me-downs. But most importantly, I would have a tattoo on my right arm, and everyone would know I was now a Scorpion. Someone to be looked up to, someone to be treated with respect, or pay the consequences. The choice would be theirs.

I'm going to the meeting tonight, I haven't been invited, but from a conversation I overheard in a backstreet bar last night in Palermo, I have worked out where they will be. This is my last chance, my last throw of the dice, so to speak.

This time tomorrow, the whole of Borgetto will have heard that I am now a Scorpion. Everyone will look up to me, especially the older men sitting outside the bars playing La Scopa. They will take time out from their card game. Their colourful banter will momentarily cease as they look up at me and nod. My name will resound through the narrow streets of Bogetto "Bravo Carinu. You make us proud." One of them will surely offer me his wine or his beer. Invite me to sit and watch a few hands of cards. I will decline. I will have better things to do with my time.

I am so nervous. The journey into Palermo seemed to take forever. I could feel myself getting worked up. My hands became sweaty, as did the back of my neck. Angello, my best friend, had driven me here. He had borrowed his father's old truck, probably without permission, but at least we were here in one piece.

The bar was down a little street. It was well away from the hustle and bustle of the busy city centre. I had to ask several people before one of them could point us in the right direction. We both noticed the strange look he gave us as he explained the quickest route. He also turned away and retraced his steps. Wherever he was going, he suddenly had a change of heart.

Angello didn't want to come in, but I persuaded him. I told him not to get involved, to just sit quietly with a drink and wait for me. Reluctantly, he agreed, and we walked in together. The room was dimly lit. It was full of young men talking and drinking until they saw us.

Five, or six of them, were over to the door, blocking us from entering within seconds. "It's a private function tonight, guys." One of them said abruptly, holding his hand close to my face. I stood my ground. I wasn't going to be intimidated that easily. I was expecting it to be hostile. I was well-prepared for a few punks to try and impress their boss. I took a deep breath and introduced myself.

"I am Carinu Russo from Borgetto. My friend here is Angello Messina. I have come to speak with your caporegime." He leaned his head to one side and smiled. An uneasy feeling rippled through my body. As his face tightened, the smile turned to a sneer, and a little snigger left his lips as he spoke. "You want to see the Capo? Don't we all?" He turned around laughing and gestured with his hands. Everyone in the room joined in, except for Angello and me. We both just looked straight ahead, not daring to move a muscle.

"Carinu Russo from Borgetto." He turned back to face me. "It has a nice ring to it. Perhaps your family should have it inscribed on your gravestone?" He clapped his hands several times at his stupid remark and turned back to the room again. There was more cheering and laughter, all at my expense. I took another deep breath. I was about to make my challenge.

"I do not have time for this! I wish to speak with whoever is in charge about joining the Scorpions." The room fell deathly silent. I was aware that my friend, Angello, had taken a step back. My best friend was distancing himself from me. I suddenly felt very alone, but I was still feeling strong.

I folded my arms in defiance and looked straight into the aggressive face of the young man barring my way.

"That last word, alone, is enough for me to make it your final word, Carinu Russo." I heard the shuffling of chairs as others behind him stood up. Heavy footsteps and murmuring voices closed in all around me. Angello might have abandoned me, but he wasn't part of this.

"My friend Angello only drove me here. He has no interest in what I want. Let him leave!"

"For someone just about to be ripped apart, Carinu Russo, you show spirit." The words reached my ears simultaneously as the many hands did. I was grabbed by my arms and legs and lifted into the air. Someone punched me in the kidneys, making my eyes sting and water.

"Enough... Enough." A harsh voice bellowed loud above the melee. Everyone in the room stopped jostling me. I was still being held aloft as they waited for further instructions. "Put him down and back away." I landed awkwardly on my feet and had to grab a chair to steady myself.

"Thank you," I said, straightening up and directing my attention to the voice at the back of the room. An older man, perhaps seventy or seventy-five, sauntered toward me. He had a mop of thick grey hair. His face was weather-beaten, brown, wrinkled, and leathery. He had seen life to the full. He shrugged his shoulders at me as if to say. "We will see."

"You are either very brave or rather foolish, walking in here making demands like that." I stretched myself up, trying to gain a little more height. I knew deep down that I wasn't fooling anyone, but I needed to do something, and I needed to do it now. I offered him my hand. "I am Carinu Russo from Borgetto… And you are?" I heard a few gasps from those around me. He ignored my hand and just stared straight into my face.

"I am," he hesitated and thought for a second. "I am your worst nightmare, young Russo. I am the one who determines your fate." He hunched his shoulders and gestured with his hands as he smirked back at me. I stood silently, looking at his face. Inside, my body was trembling, but I was determined not to let him see that.

"I came all this way because I wish to be a Scorpion. I want to do more with my life. Back home, there is nothing for me. I have spent weeks coming into Palermo at night, trying to trace where you meet and hang out. And now I am here, and I ask for a chance to be one of you!" I nodded back and mouthed a yes quietly. The older man looked impressed. He almost smiled.

"And what exactly do you think you can offer us?" He asked, leaning closer to my face to make his point. I didn't budge. I wanted to, but I kept my nerve.

"I will do anything that you ask of me. There isn't a task that I cannot perform." I spoke proudly and knew I had the whole room's attention.

"Anything?" He repeated, pursing his lips, waiting for my reply.

"Anything," I reassured him. "You name it. I will do it."

"Do you have the balls to do anything I ask?" He sounded unconvinced.

"I wish to be a Scorpion. I will do whatever it takes. Whatever is needed to fulfill my dream."

He stepped closer and placed a hand on my shoulder. He leaned into my neck. I could feel his hot breath close to my ear. "I have the perfect test for you." He whispered.

"Then tell me, so I may prove myself to you," I replied quietly enough that no one else could hear.

After his first four words, everything else sounded muffled. My head was reeling in disbelief. "Do I need to repeat that?" He whispered, looking straight into my eyes. I shook my head. I knew that I had heard him correctly.

He nodded back at me and patted the sides of my face before pinching both of my cheeks gently. "Good. We understand each other." He stepped away from me and called across the room. "Roberto. Take Carinu into the back room. He needs a piece. Give him my old one. Also, give him your mobile number. He will need to make contact with you afterwards. Showing us proof."

Roberto led me into the tiny room behind the bar. I felt dazed, and nothing was making any sense. Once the door was closed, I just stood there looking around me. There were cases of wine and crates of beer. A single old, rickety chair and a little desk were leaning up against the far wall.

"Wait there," Roberto ordered, pointing down to my feet. I watched him as he walked around the desk. He withdrew a handgun, opened the chamber, and removed several shells. He looked across at me. "You will only need the one." He clenched the bullets and shook his fist at me. "We can't trust you until you have done the hit. Then, and only then, will we invite you back here. Fail, and we will come and hunt you down like a dog."

I watched him walk towards me, swivelling the gun by the trigger guard. Showing off and probably testing me all at the same time. I stood my ground. Even when he pointed it at me, I just stared straight at him. "Bang." He shouted. I didn't flinch. I was expecting it. That's precisely what I would have done in his situation.

"Very good Carinu Russo from Borgetto. Perhaps the boss is right about you? I am not so sure, and I will wait before I make my mind up." He thrust the gun into my hand, and I stuffed it into my jacket pocket. I turned to the door to leave.

"No, not that way. Follow me." He walked to the opposite corner of the room. There was a tall, plain, grey looking fold up dividing screen. He pulled it to one side to reveal a small door. "I will tell your friend Angello to meet you outside." He slapped me on the back as he opened the door.

I was still taking in several deep breaths when Angello came running down the alleyway. He flung his arms around my neck. "I thought you weren't coming back. I feared the worst even when they told me you were waiting outside." We stood there in the quiet back alley, hugging the life out of each other. We both had our separate thoughts. Mine was probably more demanding.

Angello began the drive back to Borgetto in silence. He seemed preoccupied, excited almost. He was definitely in a hurry, driving too quickly, the headlights not picking out each tight bend until we were into them. He consistently fought with the steering wheel, turning it one way and then the other. I didn't know what was wrong with him. "Angello. Please slow down. You are going to get us both killed."

"You have had your fun, Carinu, and now my turn is just around the corner." He glanced at me and smiled. Gripping the dashboard, I shrugged away the remark.

At first, I couldn't work out where we were. Where had he stopped? It was so dark that I couldn't see. I certainly had no idea why he was getting out of the truck. I followed him and stood at the side of the road. We both seemed to look up at the same time. The ink-black sky was littered with tiny twinkling stars. He pointed at one the moment I chose to place the gun to the back of his head.

His crumpled body was now lying at my feet. I quickly took a picture and sent it to Roberto. Even now, looking down at him, I have no regrets. I was a Scorpion, and no one could take that from me.

I knew Di Stefano, the old goatherder, hadn't been up here in years. The mountain terrain was much too steep and treacherous for his ancient skinny legs. The last time I saw him hobbling down one of the narrow streets in Borgetto, his body was so bent forward that he saw more of the ground than the Sicilian sky.

His old drystone hut would keep me warm tonight. It was easy to find even in the dark. It was virtually straight up the narrow path, through the pine trees, from the bridge, a twenty-minute hike, no more.

No one would come up there in the dark. Tomorrow I will decide what to do next. Everything had just happened so quickly. A woman was screaming hysterically from beneath the bridge we had stopped on. Calling me by name, telling me to stop. I recognized the voice at once. It belonged to Valentina. She was Angello's girlfriend. He had called her while waiting for me.

It all makes sense now why Angello took a different route home. Why was he acting so excited? He thought he would see Valentina. He probably thought he was going to have his wicked way with her. The bridge isn't called lovers bridge without reason. The river has long dried up. I have certainly never seen any water flowing beneath, not a drop. It just makes for a nice dry, cosy place to sow a few wild seeds every now and again.

I stumbled through the open doorway of Di Stefano's old hut. I was hot and sticky. The adrenaline from the climb and my actions earlier were still pumping through my body. I slumped down, my back against the cold drywall. It felt nice, and I started to relax slowly. I felt my eyes become heavy, and my head jolted. I kept going over what had just happened. My head jerked down to my chest, and I tried desperately to stay awake. I needed to stay focused.

"You belong to me now, Carinu." I opened my eyes and looked around the small hut. The figure standing before me was dressed in a long black cloak. He had a hood pulled up, so the front almost covered his face.

"Who are you? What do you want?" My mouth was dry, and my words choked at the back of my throat. I watched as he crouched in front of me, but still, I couldn't see beyond his black hood in the darkness. It was as if he didn't own any facial features, but that was impossible.

"I am your new master. I actually want nothing from you but your soul, of course." His voice sounded full of pleasure, and he was laughing at me quietly.

"I am a Scorpion now. You don't own me. I belong with the Cosa Nostra, the Mafia, not you. I take orders only from my Capo. No one else." My voice was strong, even though my body was trembling. I could feel sweat beginning to form on my forehead. Some of the perspiration trickled down into the corners of my eyes and briefly blurred my vision.

The figure stood back up and laughed mockingly. He turned and walked to the hut opening. There was just enough light to see him turn around and face me once again.

"Believe me, Carinu, I own you and everyone like you. I will see you shortly. Perhaps in an hour or two. When you are ready, there is no rush. I know where to find you. I know exactly where you are." Without another word, he swished his long black cloak away from his body and was gone. I didn't see him leave through the door opening. I just knew that suddenly I was alone again. Feeling confused and bewildered.

I woke abruptly, needing several seconds to remember where I was. Looking through tired eyes, I remembered staggering in here last night. Di Stefano's goat hut had done its job. I was dry but not as warm as I had hoped. There was a cold misty air blowing in through the doorless opening.

"Carinu. Carinu Russo. It's the police. This is your last chance. Be sensible, and come out now. Hands on your head, and you will not be harmed."

That's what had woken me from my deep sleep. I stood quickly and looked around the small circular building.

"You are completely surrounded. Come out peacefully. Don't do anything stupid." Who was he to tell me what to do? I was a Scorpion now. I had completed my task. I picked up the gun that Roberto had given me last night, and even though I knew there were no bullets in it, without hesitating, I ran straight through the tiny opening of the goatherders hut. Aiming and directing it at the dozen or so uniformed police officers I saw standing and crouching in front of me.

Excruciating pain oozing from various parts of my chest was the last thing I remember. Before, the dark figure that had visited me last night swooped down and wrapped his black cloak around me, keeping me safe forever.

FALLEN FROM GRACE

Inspired by: LIKE A ROLLING STONE.
Performed by BOB DYLAN

Half a lifetime ago, she had everything in the world, but those days had well and truly deserted her. They had disappeared almost as quickly as they had arrived. At twenty-five, Amelia Hartman had rubbed shoulders with pop stars and movie stars alike. She was the woman of the moment. The one that all the men, and some women, wanted to spend time alone with.

Now she had nothing. Her life was empty. The silver spoon that once graced her lips was long gone, as were the lovers, the friends. Even her family had turned their backs on her. She was utterly alone, with only the voices in her head for company.

Beneath a heavy, cold December night sky, she slowly trudged through the city centre. She was pushing the rusty old shopping trolley that contained everything she now owned, which was no more than two black bin bags full of old worn-out clothes and a few items of ancient memories.

Most of the shops she passed were lit with neon lights, enticing would-be customers to call back tomorrow and spend their well-earned cash. It was nearly Christmas, and decorations were up everywhere. Large silver-winged angels with golden trumpets were strung across the busy road. Christmas trees were in abundance. Somewhere in the distance, she could hear Christmas carols being sung.

Amelia stopped in front of the art gallery window. People rushing to parties and restaurants hurried past without glancing at her. With grimy cupped hands pushed up against the glass, she could see right into the back of the studio. She recalled the time that she had once drunk complimentary champagne there. The drinks were always accessible, as was the cocaine.

The gallery owner had invited her. A young would-be artist was having his first exhibition viewing. He needed support, people looking, and showing an interest in his work. She frowned, desperately seeking his name. In the state that her life was in, she couldn't even recall what he had looked like.

Tears rolled down her cheeks as she fought with her memory to put a name to a face she could no longer see in her head. He had once been important to her, that much she remembered. Half a lifetime ago, she had several of his paintings, long gone now. She assumed to purchase cocaine. Her state of mind was such that she wasn't sure of anything.

As she pulled her hands away from her face and stepped back from the shop frontage, she glimpsed the tiny red heart tattoo nestled between her thumb and index finger on the back of her right hand. She touched it lightly and closed her eyes. It was like rubbing an Aladdin's lamp. However, no magical genie appeared to her in a wisp of smoke. Touching the red heart tattoo, she was suddenly transported back to where she wanted to be, in happier times.

"Amelia darling. I'm so pleased that you could make it. Tell me, what do you think? You know I always value your thoughts and comments." Amelia looked at the picture in question. Her first thought was, is it the right way up? The long splashes of blue and yellow that had run down the canvas mixed themselves together in a mismatch of colour.

It looked like someone had probably used a large brush to flick the paint on the canvas. Then the artist threw the remaining contents of both paint tins straight at the ever-changing picture. Leaving the dripping paint to its own devices.

"Well," she hesitated. "I think it looks upside down."

"Oh, Amelia, you are such a tease. You know it's the right way up. There's the artist's signature in the bottom right-hand corner." Lionel, the gallery owner, clapped his hands together before pointing at the white scrawl he claimed to be someone's name.

"I see it has a red paper dot on it," she said, changing the subject slightly. "It's sold then?" Amelia added knowingly.

Lionel began nodding passionately. "Almost all of them, darling. This one for 10,000 dollars. The red and white one over there," he cast an arm towards the opposite wall, "for 15,000. And we have only been open for three hours. Corey is over the moon. That said, he is probably under the table by now. He has been in the backroom for almost an hour and isn't drinking coffee. It's all been too much for him. Until today, he had never sold a single painting."

"May I?" Amelia asked, looking towards the backroom door. Lionel nodded. "Be my guest, darling. If you can get him sorted out, people with big fat wallets are dying to meet him." Amelia smiled and walked away, with no idea what would greet her.

Once inside the small storage room, she closed the door behind her and turned the key. The young artist sat with his head in his hands, murmuring obscenities under his breath. Amelia crouched in front of him, her skirt riding up past her thighs, showing her well-toned long sun-tanned legs.

"You need to get your act together. There are punters out there itching to give you money. You are doing yourself no good at all in here moping." At first, he didn't look up. Or acknowledge the soft, warm fingers that began gently rubbing the back of his neck.

"I'm not ready for this." He muttered, his hands still covering his face.

"Come on, of course you are. You're a very talented artist. But you need to be mingling, smiling, and conversing. They are your public, think of them as puppets, and you are the puppeteer pulling the strings." He dropped his hands. Amelia knew instantly from the beaming smile on his face that she had struck a chord.

He leaned forward and kissed her. "Thank you." Without another word, he was on his feet and unlocking the storeroom door. He hesitated and then turned back to face her. "I really need you on my arm," he said, offering an outstretched hand. She walked towards him, gripped his hand tightly, and they stepped out into the gallery as one.

A church clock chimed midnight. Amelia turned and looked around the now empty street. Everyone had vanished, and the pavements were deserted of all life. Amelia had lost track of time, she had no idea how long she had been standing there looking in the gallery window, reminiscing, but for the first time in a long time, she had a feeling of contentment, a warmth inside her body, that she hadn't felt in a long time.

A yellow taxi bumbled by slowly, it was going nowhere of interest, and neither was Amelia. She pulled her shabby old woollen hat further down over her ears. Suddenly everything had changed, she was now feeling the cold, and her bones ached. She blew into her hands several times before rubbing them together. She felt exhausted and drained of energy.

The gallery doorway offered her some form of shelter. She quickly pulled the two black bags out of the trolley and rummaged through them. She found the lightweight blanket and wrapped it around her thin body, but it did very little to keep her boney shoulders warm. As she sat there huddled up against the front door, she was now physically shaking with the cold. Her teeth chattering, her nose and ears stinging.

Her head was swimming, but somehow her thoughts seemed less muddled. *"We had some good times together, Corey Emerson."* The ghostly images she had seen through the gallery window had brought back long-forgotten memories. That first meeting, and how she had known exactly how she felt about this young struggling artist in a matter of minutes.

"Such a shame our paths weren't destined to stay

together. That was down to me, I guess. I was the one hungry for fame. I was the one that the rich and famous wanted on their arm and in their bed. You were only just starting out, and I couldn't wait for you. I was also very hurtful to you. I'm sorry, Corey." Amelia shuddered at her own unkind words and slowly closed her eyes.

In her thoughts, people came and went. The well-known politician from Capitol Hill and his stupid bodyguard, whose job was to stand on the other side of the door of the seedy motel room they always used. Assurance that they wouldn't be disturbed, he had called it. As was the norm, she was always the first to leave, and he gave her the same easy-to-read grin on his face, which told her he could hear every sound they made.

Then there was the lead singer of a famous chart-topping rock band, whose habit was to flick his long dark hair off his shoulders when showing his frustration. It was always the same discussion between the drummer and the guitarists as to who was snorting the lines of coke and who was joining them both on the giant round waterbed.

Everything was passing through her head on a conveyor belt of dreams. The day Corey arrived unannounced, pleading with her to take him back. *"Those days are gone."* She had told him. In desperation, he had threatened to shoot himself. She had nastily offered to buy him the gun. She never saw or heard from him again. But without him and his support, it was the start of her fall from grace.

The temperature had dropped dramatically during the night, and heavy snow had fallen. The early morning sun struggled to shine. It was no more than an opaque ball hanging in a translucent sky. But at least the city was waking up. All be it slowly. People were taking care not to slip on pavements, walking gingerly and holding onto railings and streetlights as they ventured out.

Cars and buses were manoeuvring carefully on the slushy, icy grey roads. The drivers took care to avoid skidding into the vehicles parked at the kerb, some already abandoned by frustrated drivers. Life in the city was generally on the go slow.

The cold air burnt and stung his cheeks. His white breath rose and then quickly disappeared into the cold air. He would have stayed home, but the gallery was preparing for a new exhibition. Various sizes of sculptures and canvases were arriving throughout the day if, of course, the couriers could get through the city in the first place. The other main factor was whether the snow was going to keep away.

The early morning forecast hadn't been good, it was just a matter of time before the heavens opened and New York would possibly experience its heaviest snowfall in decades. Only time would tell. In the meanwhile, life had to go on as best it could.

The ten-minute walk from the warehouse, which had long ago been converted into his studio, come home had taken half an hour. He turned the corner and saw the crowd gathered outside the gallery. He checked his watch. They weren't due to open for another hour, Hattie, his young assistant, might be there by now, but she wouldn't let people in before time. He quickened his pace.

"Excuse me. I need to get through," he shouted, trying to move people aside.

"I think she's dead?" He heard a woman's voice nearer the door of the gallery. His first thoughts were of Hattie, had she slipped on unseen ice beneath the snow?

"Would you please let me through? I own this gallery. And I need to get in." At that moment, a police officer stood up. He had been crouching in the doorway, his body masked by all the bystanders.

"I'm afraid I can't allow that, sir. We have a fatality here." As he spoke, some of the crowd automatically dispersed. They now knew the verdict. They weren't much interested in anything else. A corpse, was a corpse, was a corpse.

He could now see the slumped body blocking his doorway, he knew at once that it wasn't his assistant Hattie, and a wave of relief washed over him. From the body size, he guessed the dead person was female, obviously, homeless by her appearance. Even though he didn't know her, his heart went out to her. There were times in his life when he could so easily have been here himself.

The police officer went back to examining the lifeless body. He checked the two black bags but found nothing of interest. Behind him, the curiosity of the crowd was wearing thin. Most of them had better things to do. Most of those on their way to work didn't even bother to think about who the woman was. What had really happened to her? To them, she was just another statistic. Something that had happened to someone else and not to them. Something of interest to talk about with their colleagues when they arrive at their workplace.

"She has no identification on her. Another Jane Doe, I'm afraid. This is my second one this week. There are times when I hate this job." The officer sounded sincere as he looked at the few remaining people.

The sound of a wailing siren broke into the remaining onlooker's thoughts. Some turned to watch, while others just stood there staring. As the vehicle pulled outside the gallery, the experienced officer automatically entered crowd control mode. He spread his arms out and stepped carefully backwards, allowing the two medics to get through.

"It's all over, folks. There's nothing more to see. Mind how you go." His words had the desired effect. Everyone except the gallery owner left the scene.

After a quick check by one of the medics, they carefully lifted the lifeless body onto the lightweight metal gurney. In doing so, the corpse's right hand flopped down from beneath the white shroud. The gallery owner saw it immediately. "Officer. I can identify this woman." His voice was quiet, almost a whisper.

"And exactly how can you do that, sir?" He replied sceptically. The officer watched as the gallery owner pointed to the faded tattoo on the back of her hand. The police officer leaned forward and took a closer look.

"It's a red heart." He replied, shrugging his shoulders.

"Her name is Amelia Hartman."

"And you know that because...?" The officer asked sceptically.

The gallery owner pulled up his coat sleeve and revealed his own little red heart on the back of his right hand.

"My name's Corey Emerson. I was once a struggling artist. I had my first exhibition here. But now, I'm a successful art dealer in my own right. I now own the place that kicked started my career. But I would never have made it without Amelia Hartman. She helped me through my bouts of depression. My drinking and my insatiable appetite for drugs. I probably owe her my life."

"You will need to come down to the station and make a full statement Mr. Emerson."

"Yes, of course. Tell me, what will happen to Amelia now? I know she has no family."

"Well, I suppose name-wise, it's a little bit ironic, really. She will be kept on ice for a few days while we await a coroner's report. Plus, we will need to make a few other checks. And then the body will be shipped to Hart Island." He pointed in the direction of the water, which was not visible because of all the tall buildings. It's located at the western end of Long Island Sound. It's where all the unclaimed bodies end up."

Corey Emerson was already shaking his head. "No, no, that can't happen. I can't allow Amelia to be laid to rest in a paupers grave. She deserves a proper burial, and I will see to that. I owe her that and so much more."

"Hey, Mackenzie." One of the two medics stopped and turned. "Mr. Emerson here needs a lift. He knows the deceased woman." The medic nodded and waved him forward to sit in the front with them.

"Forty ninth Precinct, don't forget. Ask for officer Warren." Corey Emerson raised an arm as he hurried after the medic. "Thank you, officer Warren.

I'll be there."

"Good luck Mr. Emerson." He muttered under his breath just as a young woman with bright green shoulder-length hair approached him.

"And from the description, I assume you are Hattie, Mr. Emerson's young assistant."

"I am. What is going on?"

"Well, you missed the main event. But I believe you have a busy day ahead of you. Any chance of a quick coffee, and I'll explain everything." He saw Hattie look at the abandoned trolley.

"Yes, I'll explain that as well." He added.

THE BRIDGE

Inspired by: WATERLOO SUNSET.
Performed by THE KINKS

Danny hurried through the city streets, stepping one way and then another to avoid the busy commuters making their way home. Friday evenings always seemed to be the busiest. They all had a single thought, reach sanctuary before the heavens opened.

In the capital, the last rays of the evening sun had dropped behind a landscape of famous landmarks and some of the other tall sprawling office buildings. The night sky seemed to change instantly, as heavy rolling clouds full of threatening rain replaced the evening glow. Thunder rumbled further down the river, warning everyone that the rain was imminent, now just moments away.

Someone caught his shoulder as they passed him. It sent him sideways, he spun around, but there was no acknowledgment of the clash. He cursed and rubbed the top of his arm. It was still sore from where he had been kicked in the early hours of the morning. He automatically touched his cheek, which he knew was still red and swollen.

The four lads had woken him up and set about him, calling him a lazy scumbag. Then they had beaten him until a man came running down the side street, yelling and screaming for them to stop. They had laughed and sworn at Danny's saviour, but they still ran away. Turning occasionally and shouting more obscenities. Brave until the last.

The stranger had helped him to his feet and advised him to go to a hospital for a check-up. He had said he would, knowing full well that that was a lie. His ribs hurt, and his face was splattered with blood. He could feel his right eye swelling up and closing by the second.

This was the third time he had been set upon in as many weeks, but this was by far the worst beating he had ever taken. Why did so many individuals despise homeless people? They didn't know the circumstances. They didn't know if it was their fault or not. But still, they were labelled as scroungers and parasites. Lazy, good for nothings, living on handouts, smoking themselves to death, taking drugs. People knew nothing about them. They were just too quick to surmise.

Danny had slowed his pace. The barge to the shoulder had taken the wind out of him. His legs suddenly felt like lead, and everything ached to the extreme. Even his rucksack, which was virtually empty, felt heavy on his back. He stopped with all the other pedestrians on the edge of the pavement and waited for the lights to say that it was safe for him to cross the busy road. He was grateful for the respite.

The green walking man lit up, and he heard the familiar beeping sound that indicated it was safe to go. He hurried across the road and headed for the bridge. Sanctuary was in his sights. He would wait for

T.J. as he always did at the start of the weekend. This was their special get-together. It happened every Friday night, and he looked forward to it so much.

From where he had been waiting patiently for the last few minutes, he watched the ever-changing rippled effects of the bridge lights reflecting across the water below him. Changing yet again as the first large splodges of rain descended onto the river. He pulled his collar high around his neck. How much longer should he wait?

She was never late. Even the threat of rain had never put her off before. Where was she? What had happened? Something had, of that he was sure. The wailing siren of an ambulance pierced the silence that surrounded him. He turned in response and watched as it sped across the bridge away from him, blue lights illuminating the night sky.

"Poor girl," a woman said to her friend as they walked past him chatting. "She looked so young. What on earth made her jump?"

"I only saw the back of her. It was just a blur of long blue hair trailing over the edge and down into the water."

"So sad."

Danny's heart almost stopped. Everything was spinning around in his head. She was late. The ambulance rushing by hadn't helped. Worst of all, T.J. had long blue hair. She had told him last week that she found the squeezy bottle in a bin. He suspected that she had probably stolen it from a shop somewhere.

His heart pounded as he stood looking along the length of the bridge. He knew, deep down, he knew. He wanted to run after the disappearing vehicle and see for himself. But he didn't move. He still believed deep down that she would come. She always did. She had to come.

This was the place that she loved most in all the world. Her special bridge. To Danny, it was just a way of crossing the busy river. He had never even considered it to be an attractive-looking bridge. To him, it was nothing more than reinforced concrete doing a job.

T.J. thought differently. She loved walking across it with him. They always strolled arm in arm, laughing and giggling at nothing, catching up on their days apart, watching how the people passing stared at them, making judgements without understanding. No one knew anything about them. In their eyes, they were just two scruffy homeless individuals walking the streets.

No one knew the circumstances that had driven them both here. Her drunken mother had thrown her out because she complained about all the different men that came and went. Some of them even tried to hit on her, but her mother hadn't listened, and when she was told to leave, she didn't hesitate. She packed what few things she wanted and walked out the front door.

The rain had eased now, but his thoughts certainly hadn't. Everything inside his head was an assortment of desperate ideas. He had played out every scenario, and none of them had made any sense. He was anxious, hopeless, and uptight. Close to doing something stupid. Every muscle and nerve in his body was wound up tighter than a clock spring. One more turn of the key…

Tonight, there was no flaming red setting sun. On the left, he could see the London Eye, all lit up, changing colour periodically, as the wheel slowly turned. He could even see Big Ben. None of these were of any interest to him. Jumping and ending it all was the only thing on his mind. T.J. was gone. He had heard the women say as much. There was nothing left for him now.

"You alright up there, buddy?" Danny half turned to face the inquiring voice. The man was a white-collar worker, a businessman. Smart dark suit, flashy bright tie, probably on his way home to his pleasant warm abode. Even though the rain had ceased, he still held up an umbrella. Danny ignored the question. Instead, he shrugged his shoulders without bothering to reply. His head was still fuzzy, his thoughts a jumbled mess.

"Pretty crap weather for June. More rain forecast tomorrow as well, so they say." The voice behind him carried on, interrupting his thoughts.

"Really! I can't say I'm much bothered one way or the other." He replied eventually, still staring down but seemingly straight through the man standing there looking up at him.

"Summers aren't like they used to be. Climate change and all that." The stranger talked about nothing, hoping that the situation might suddenly change for the better, that the young man would come down from the ledge and everything would be okay. He made one more final attempt to make some contact.

"Don't do it. She's not worth it."

"Don't do what? Who's not worth it?"

"You know, jump. Whoever she is, she's not worth you taking your life for."

"I'm homeless and destitute. And now, completely alone." His voice was raised and angry. The businessman removed his phone from his jacket pocket. Danny heard the rhythmic tapping of keys and realised what he was doing.

"They won't get here in time. No one can help me now. My life is over."

"Yea, sorry. Nothing to do with me. I've put my phone away. But couldn't we talk about it, just you and me?"

"Her name was T.J. If you must know." he hesitated. "She was homeless like me, and now she's gone. She was supposed to meet me here, but she hasn't."

The businessman managed a smile. He felt pleased with himself. He had made a breakthrough, progress of sorts. "She probably sheltered in some shop doorway, waiting for the storm to pass." He watched the man shake his head, causing water droplets to run down his face and mingle in his unkempt beard.

"No, like me, the rain doesn't bother her. This is our home." He held his hands aloft and pointed up and down the bridge. "Here, over there on the other side of the road. In a way, all of this is our home." The businessman nodded, making out that he understood.

"I sometimes wish that she was my girlfriend, though. We looked out for each other. We got on really well." The businessman saw the change in the young man. He suddenly looked lost. His head bowed, his shoulders hunched.

"My name's Jacob, by the way. Most people call me Jake." He said, ignoring the girlfriend reference.

"Danny. I'm Danny."

"Well, Danny. I think she will be here soon. I think my idea that she sheltered was right. The rain has stopped, and now she's on her way. You wait and see." Jacob smiled; he was making progress and enjoying trying to be the good Samaritan.

"I don't think that is going to happen, Jake. T.J. won't be coming. Not today or any other day." Danny slowly turned back towards the river. Jacob could see the pained look in his eyes.

"She will come, Danny. It's destined that you two should be together. It's written in the stars." Danny stopped and thought about the remark. He began to nod his head.

"T.J. was always talking about stars and galaxies far away. She used to say that if we stand here on warm summer evenings, watching the fiery sky in the distance. And see a shooting star, that it was a message from another world. She believed in aliens and all that." Jacob wanted to laugh out loud. Instead, he changed the subject slightly.

"So, how did you two meet?" He asked, stepping closer to the parapet.

"I was, according to her, sitting on her pitch. She told me in no uncertain terms to clear off. I stood up, picked up my blanket, and started to walk off. But she didn't let me go. Instead, she grabbed me by my arm and stopped me. Then she asked."

"What Zodiac sign are you? My guess is, you're an Aquarian?"

"I remember looking confused because she

was right, and I didn't know how she knew. I wanted to get away."

"You are a bloody Aquarian, aren't you?"

"I was annoyed and said the first thing that came into my head. No, I'm a Leo, actually."

"Liar. Leos are strong. You're not a Leo."

"Yes, okay, you're right. I'm an Aquarian. Happy now? Then she hugged me and kissed me."

"I love Aquarians."

"She replied excitedly and invited me to sit down with her on her pitch."

"Wow, that's a lovely story, Danny. Why don't you come down? We could go for a warm drink. Sit somewhere in the dry, and you could tell me more about her."

Danny suddenly became agitated. He pointed an accusing finger at Jacob. "You just told me that she was coming. That she had sheltered and that she was on her way. Now you want me to leave with you and miss her."

"Danny. Danny. That's not what I meant. I meant that if you came down, we could wait for her. All three of us could go for a drink and a bite to eat."

"Don't you have a nice warm home to go to?" Danny was still angry, his voice loud and hostile.

"What's going on here?" Someone asked from behind Jacob's back. He turned to face two middle-aged women. They were standing, both holding supermarket carrier bags. Danny, at once, recognised them from earlier. They were the ones who had started all of this without realising it.

"It's okay," Jacob tried to reassure them. The last thing he wanted was for one of them to start panicking and become flustered. To spook Danny any more than he already was. To make matters worse, four other people crossed the road to see what was happening. A crowd was beginning to gather as someone else appeared and stood watching.

"This is the second time tonight." One of the women with the shopping said, sounding exasperated. Jacob frowned, and she saw his questioning expression.

"A young woman jumped off this bridge less than twenty minutes ago. Up the other end. We were there." Both women nodded simultaneously. Reality slowly dawned on Jacob.

"Nothing we could do. She was gone in a second."

"We dialled 999 and waited. A police officer arrived on foot first, quickly followed by an ambulance." The larger of the two women added.

"We couldn't tell him very much. I noticed her rolled-up jeans and her blue hair. That was about it. Poor girl."

Danny's body tensed. T.J. always rolled her jeans up at the bottoms. She didn't like anything around her ankles.

"Maureen and I disagreed about her hair, though. I thought it was more of a green colour."

"Green, blue. Whatever." Maureen added as though it didn't matter anymore.

T.J. hesitated when she saw the people gathered on the bridge. She stood on tiptoe to get a better look. She gasped when she saw the figure standing on the parapet's edge, leaning over, looking down into the dark swirling water.

Danny slowly removed his tatty old rucksack from his back and held it over the edge. He was utterly oblivious to the people standing behind him. T.J. took several steps forward, telling a man in front of her that she knew him. She knew the jumper. Jacob moved aside, allowing her through.

"Dan, it's T.J. please get down." She spoke to him as calmly as she could, almost inferring that there was no danger, nothing to worry about. He half turned on hearing her voice. She saw him smile, his brown eyes showing the pleasure he felt seeing her.

"I thought you were...I thought that something had happened to you. That you weren't coming." He shuffled his feet around on the narrow ledge to face her. Several onlookers held their breath. The rain had made the concrete slippery once false move, and he was gone.

"I stopped for coffees, look see. A sweet young man gave me a tenner." She held the two polystyrene cups up for him to see.

"You always were better at begging than me." He replied.

"Who cares? We are a team, Dan."

She watched in terror as he turned back to face the water below him.

"Danny. I love you. Please get down so that we can have our drink."

Without warning, eight or nine pigeons suddenly flew up from beneath one of the bridge arches. Two nearly hit him, their flapping wings narrowly missing his face. He jerked backwards to avoid them both. T.J. screamed and dropped both of the coffees. She automatically jumped to avoid the hot liquid, and her hands flew up to her face, covering her eyes.

In that split second, she heard a loud splash

and yelled "No!" at the top of her voice. She stood motionless. She didn't want to look, but she knew she had to. Slowly she lowered her hands and saw Danny, leaning as far forward as he dared.

"Everything I owned in the world was in there. Those bloody pigeons have cost me my rucksack." He pivoted on the wet ledge and stared back at T.J. "You as well? I was looking forward to that coffee." He was smiling and trying to keep his balance at the same time. The bystanders held their breath as his arms see-sawed up and down as he tried to adjust his weight.

Once settled, he jumped down and straight into her arms. "Did you say you loved me?" He asked, holding her tightly. Jacob couldn't control his emotions. He clapped loudly, some of the applause aimed at himself.

Maureen's friend nudged her in the ribs. "Like I said. Her hair was green. That is definitely blue." They walked away smiling. Others followed some disappointed that the outcome wasn't what they expected.

THE COLORADO MOTEL

Inspired by: HOTEL CALIFORNIA.
Performed by THE EAGLES

I knew that I was going to be the last to arrive. Lee and Callum sent me text messages earlier in the day to say they were there waiting for me. It was nearly dark when my taxi pulled up outside. The last glow of the desert sun was slowly dropping behind a backdrop of tall, rugged mountains in the distance. The Mexican cab driver seemed in a hurry to be on his way. He took my money but looked as nervous as hell and drove away quicker than we arrived. I thought no more of it. In hindsight, that was probably my first mistake.

I expected to see both of my rock-climbing buddies standing at the main entrance, each with a bottle of Bud in their hand and, hopefully, one for me. There was no one to be seen. I slung my rucksack over one shoulder and headed for the only light I could see. A strong dry wind suddenly whipped sand up around my legs. The temperature dropped, and the cold air made me shudder.

Like something out of a Hitchcock movie, the main door creaked and groaned as I slowly and now nervously pushed it open.

"Hello... Hi. Is there anyone here?" Seconds

passed, and I was still standing there wondering what had happened to everyone. Hearing every little squeak and scratch of the wooden interior was jangling on my nerves. Mice, lizards, rattlesnakes, my mind was running riot.

"Good evening, sir." The voice from behind me almost forced my heart up into my mouth. I turned to face a man probably about my age, early thirties. After that, there were no other similarities. He was thin and bony, his black hair receding from his forehead, revealing pale white skin that looked like it had never seen the light of day. "Greetings from the Colorado Motel. Do you have a reservation?" His crooked teeth were yellowed, and his over-plump lips were wet, almost to the point that he was dribbling.

"Yes," I replied. "I'm here with two of my friends. We're the rock climbers. We booked it last week. Well, Callum did. I remember he said that he spoke with a woman. She sounded elderly. Perhaps your mother?" He was already shaking his head. "My mother passed away several years ago, sir. We also don't have any women working here. Just me, I'm Harvey and Curtis. He's my brother and also the chief."

"Well, both my buddies are here somewhere. They texted to say that they had arrived. I've just flown in from Denver. I arrived at Alamosa airport and caught a taxi straight here." He was still shaking his head at me. His eyes seemingly, rolling around in their deep-set sockets.

"Rock, climbing, you said? We don't get any rock climbers here. Too isolated. Nothing around here for miles." I watched as he slapped the top of his balding head. The action indicating that somewhere inside him, a light bulb had just come on.

"I bet my last bottom dollar that you and your rock-climbing friends have booked into the Colorado Hotel. Hotel, Motel, it nearly sounds the same." Spending many happy hours on my phone and laptop, I didn't need to check where the two first starting letters were on the keyboards. I could almost visualise Callum's index finger hitting the wrong button.

"So, how far are we from the hotel?" I asked, feeling frustrated.

"Thirty minutes in daylight, maybe fifty-five in the dark," Harvey informed me, not sounding sorry about my predicament.

"What happens now?" I asked, sounding agitated.

"Well, you won't get anyone coming out here after dark. There's a stiff wind blowing up, and there will be dust and sand everywhere. Visibility will be down to zero by now, that's for sure."

"Great! So, I'm stuck here?" I let that sink in for a few seconds before dropping my rucksack to the floor and stretching out a hand. "I'm Kelvin Garret. Pleased to meet you." Harvey's hand was cold and clammy, and I couldn't get it out of mine quickly enough.

I walked over to the window. It was pitch black out there, but I was aware of the invisible grains of sand pinging on the dirty glass pane. Deep down, I knew that I wasn't going anywhere tonight.

"How's about a beer? I'm sure we can work something out." He pointed to another door and beckoned that I follow him. "This is the bar and lounge area. Good old comfy seats. We've even got us a dartboard." He said it with such passion and pride as he turned around the dingy room.

The bar was no longer than six feet in length. On the back wall, there were two optics, both containing the same brand of whiskey. Both were nearly empty. The comfy seats were certainly old and very faded. So much so that I couldn't tell what colour the fabric had been originally. The chill cabinet wasn't much better. The front glass door was cracked so badly that you couldn't see the contents inside.

Harvey saw the pained expression on my face as I squinted. "Oh, we got Dale's Pale Ale in there." He pointed at the cabinet, grinning enthusiastically at me.

"What else do you have?" I asked, following him towards the bar.

"Nothing. Just Dale's. You can't beat Oskar Blues Brewery. They make the best beer in the county." I closed my eyes and bit my bottom lip. I struggled to keep my opinions civil, but I was here and going nowhere fast, so be polite, I told myself. And then I repeated twice more before asking for a can of Dale's Pale Ale.

I reluctantly settled down in the lounge. Harvey had gone to check out one of the rooms for me to sleep in. Probably to fumigate it and to tell the cockroaches to keep the noise down. The sofa I chose nearly sank to the floor when I sat on it. There were no springs and, indeed, no padding for support.

At least the beer was cold. I sipped a little more and wondered why I hadn't heard from either Lee or Callum. Surely, they must be wondering where I was by now. My vivid imagination conjured up a picture of them both standing at the right bar in the

Colorado Hotel, enjoying a bottle of Bud accompanied by a whiskey chaser. Not worrying a rat's arse that I was stranded somewhere else and all on my lonesome. Drinking pale ale from a dirty glass and wondering if things could get any worse?

Harvey returned, rubbing his hands together and grinning madly. "You're in luck. Curtis has agreed to rustle you up some food. Ten minutes tops." He added, still seeming pleased with himself.

"My friends haven't called me yet. Very frustrating," I said without looking up from my phone.

"Oh, you won't get a signal in this storm. Best wait until the morning, when it's all blown over." Harvey was standing over me, hovering like a praying mantis waiting to strike at any second. We both looked up when the door was flung open. A tall, thick-set man walked in carrying my tray of food. He introduced himself as Curtis, and at least his hand was firm and dry. He said something to Harvey about *she's done*, but it was nothing to do with me, so I thought no more of it.

He placed the tray on a small table in front of me, and suddenly, I had two praying mantises watching me. It was very unnerving. I wanted to say something, but Curtis came to my rescue. "Harv, he doesn't have a knife and fork." While his brother scurried away like a two-legged rodent, I looked at the food. Curtis was eyeballing me, watching my every expression.

"Deep fried nuggets, with a hot chilli dip." He explained. "A healthy portion of fries, kale, and sliced avocado. Plenty of vitamins and iron in there for you." Curtis had the same leering grin as his brother when he spoke. He wiped his greasy hands down his jeans and eventually stepped away.

I waited for Harvey to return. The knife and fork were wet when he handed them to me, so I guessed he had to wash them through. By now, I was starving. The flight from Denver was just under an hour, so I only had time for coffee and a snack on board.

I dived straight into one of the nuggets, it was a bit chewy but tasty, and I realised that the brothers were watching my every move. I saw Harvey nudge Curtis as I devoured my second nugget loaded with the hot chilli dip. Another can of beer appeared on the small table. I looked up and nodded my thanks to Harvey before carrying on eating.

Both brothers had retired to the bar and were standing waiting as I placed my cutlery on the clean plate. I walked over to them. "That was delicious," I said, wiping my mouth on a paper napkin. Curtis began to nod.

"Glad you enjoyed it. Young rattlers always taste better. The flesh is softer." He was grinning, clearly enjoying every moment." I Laughed. I knew he was joking with me. He lifted something off the bar. "Say, do you want to keep the rattle? It won't sound as good as when it was on the snake. No man alive can shake that fast." He was still smiling and now, shaking the rattlesnake's tail in the air, making a dull waka-waka noise. My chicken nuggets, which were no longer chicken nuggets, were now asking to be released from my stomach.

Harvey walked over to retrieve my plate. "If you want a room, which I assume you do? Plus, your supper, that will be thirty dollars, cash. How does that sound?" Expensive, I thought, but I kept my mouth firmly closed, knowing how the nuggets were feeling. I raised my thumb to indicate that it was fine. He smiled. He knew damn well I was struggling, and he loved every moment.

I watched him leave with Curtis in tow. I swear they were both giggling like a couple of naughty schoolchildren. I tried to contact the guys again, but there was still no reception. So, here I was, stuck in the middle of nowhere. With two weird brothers who liked serving their guest rattlesnake with fries. Do I want to hang around for breakfast? Probably not.

Harvey had returned, still drooling and flashing his crooked yellow teeth at me.
"Your room is ready, sir. Shall I take your bag?" I struggled out of the deep hollow of the sofa like a three-year-old trying to get out of a deckchair on the beach. He had already picked up my rucksack and was way ahead of me.

We passed door after door, some with numbers on, others showing faded outlines where the number had once been. Surely all of these rooms weren't taken? I asked myself as we trudged along the narrow, dimly lit hallway. Eventually, he stopped and turned the brass doorknob. "There isn't any hot water until tomorrow morning, I'm afraid. Sleep well." He handed me my rucksack and was gone without a second glance. At least the light switch worked.

The room was small and looked like it had once been used for storage rather than sleeping in. A single bed just fitted in lengthways against one wall. The room's only natural light was a tiny fan window above the headboard. A tall wooden wardrobe with a full-length mirror and a silver-looking handle stood behind the main door. It was empty of everything, including clothes hangers. Welcome to paradise Kelvin Garret, I said to myself before collapsing on the bed.

I was still not convinced that I couldn't get a signal. But the phone knew better. I played around with it for ten minutes or so. I typed messages to both the guys, telling them where I was. Blaming Callum for being stuck out here in the middle of nowhere. Generally sounding pissed off. After every message, my phone pinged me back, indicating that it hadn't gone. It was queued, waiting its turn.

I lay there staring at the ceiling, my eyes were desperate for sleep, but my head and thoughts were wide awake. I was in this mess because I chose to stay at work and not make the long drive to Colorado with Callum and Lee. Had I done the right thing, we would all be together now. Sharing a few beers, eating out, laughing, joking, and planning our attack on Crestone Needle. Plotting which trails we were going to take over the next few days.

Callum and Lee have climbed Crestone Needle and the higher, more difficult Crestone Peak several times. For me, it was going to be a first. The adventure of a lifetime, or so I thought. But without them knowing my whereabouts and no contact from either side. I doubted that they were going to hang around waiting for me. It would all be over for me unless I did something positive.

I checked the time. It was two fifteen. I had been lying on my bed for over four hours, but it seemed like only a few minutes. Perhaps I had nodded off at some time? Now I was straining and concentrating on the storm outside. I couldn't hear anything, so I guessed it had stopped. I quickly rechecked my phone, which indicated that I had a weak signal, just two bars. Maybe I could get a better signal outside. Even find some higher ground, but do something. Anything was better than being stretched out on this bed, feeling sorry for myself.

The hallway was unnervingly quiet. I hesitated and looked at my phone again, which had moved to three bars. Things were getting better by the minute. Closing the bedroom door gently, I strolled along the narrow passage. I was purposely moving away from the lounge and the front door area. I knew there had been no signal there earlier, and now I was banking on finding a back door and higher ground outside.

The hallway turned sharp to the right. I was in a long passageway, where the lights were flickering, threatening to go out at any second. It made me hurry, I'm generally not afraid of the dark, but this was spooky. It felt as if the walls were getting narrower, and they were closing in on me.

In the gloomy distance, I could hear a low humming sound. A generator, perhaps, that sound of noise. I quickened my pace. My legs felt like they wanted to run, but my head ruled and kept me walking at a steady rate.

It turned out to be a small, compact, purpose-built cold storage room. The temperature monitor on the wall read minus twenty-five degrees Celsius. Curiosity got the better of me. The big thick metal handle was extremely cold on my hand as I pulled it down. Once inside, I found the metal-clad switch and turned the light on. Three long fluorescent tubes flickered into life. The storage room was empty except for five big deep chest freezers.

On top of each freezer lid were pieces of paper held down with grey gaffer tape. Someone had written my name on one of them in red marker pen. I didn't stop to think. Grabbing the white moulded handle and using both hands, I lifted the lid. A waft of ice-cold air greeted me. It stung my face and made my eyes watery. It was empty, of course. I slammed the lid closed and hurriedly turned to leave. I needed to get out of here. In fact, I needed to get out of this whole damn building.

The name of Mary-Ann Harris on the freezer next to mine caught my eye. Curtis's words came flooding into my head like a wild tsunami. *She's done.* That's what he had said. I couldn't leave now. No matter how much my body was shaking, I needed to have a look, to see for myself. I stepped closer and hesitated, but only briefly.

I slowly lifted the freezer lid, and even through the plastic sheeting, I could see the dismembered body of a woman. That was the moment the lights went out in the storage room. I turned panic-stricken. What was happening? In that split second, my eyes must have been closed because I hadn't seen any movement in the cold changing light. All I heard was the sound of the thick metal door being slammed shut and someone on the other side of the storage room securing the padlock. I was trapped and in danger of freezing to death.

My phone suddenly pinged. I almost dropped it as my cold fingers fumbled for it in my pocket. The illuminated screen said it was Callum. His message was short and direct. "Where the hell are you!!!" I eagerly re-read the message. It had obviously been sent before my first message. Which, like his, had been delayed. Now my screen was clear, and everything I had been trying to send had gone.

My hands were becoming numb with the cold. I brought up his number and pressed the green icon. The phone rang and rang, but he still didn't answer. Now my phone told me I only had ten percent battery life. I could feel the energy draining from my body as well now, but I needed to keep going. It was almost impossible to type, but eventually, I managed, and my call for help was on its way.

I had kept it short and simple. Callum would already know where I was from my previous messages. *"Owners are madmen. Locked me in cold storage room. Freezing to death."* I wrapped my arms around my body and slapped my hands up and down in an effort to keep warm. More importantly, even in the dark, I kept moving. Sitting down wasn't an option unless I wanted to die.

My phone pinged, and again I struggled to hold it. I sighed with relief when I saw it was Callum. "Nearly there, buddy. State Troopers ahead of us. Your hosts were already under investigation. Will explain later. Hang in there." I was just about to reply with a hurry-up please message. When I heard the door being unlocked. I stepped back and watched as the heavy metal door slowly swung open, and to my horror, I saw Harvey and Curtis standing there, both holding very large cleavers.

"Thought you'd be out cold by now, Mr Garret." Curtis sneered back at me and looked at his brother. "Let's give him another hour. I'll drop the temperature down a few more degrees." As he spoke, they were already closing the storage door.

I moved as fast as I could, but it was tight shut by the time I got there. I rested a hand on the cold door and the other on the wall, and my fingers touched the light switch. At first, the three fluorescent lights protested, but eventually, they lit up the room with a dim yellow glow.

"State Troopers. Put the cleavers down, now." I didn't count the shots that were fired. I just started pounding on the metal door and yelling at the top of my voice.

ONE LIFE, ONE HEART

Inspired by: STAIRWAY TO HEAVEN.
Performed By: LED ZEPPELIN

Marjorie Cohen lay on the hospital bed staring up at the ceiling. Her eyes were almost closed from all the heavy swelling around her face. The fluorescent light above her head seemed to rise and dip as she tried to focus on it. She didn't try to move. Every single part of her body seemed to be racked with pain.

The eighteen-wheeler that hit her car at the busy intersection had careered into four other vehicles first and killed nine innocent people, including the truck driver himself. Police at the horrific scene confirmed that he was texting on his mobile phone at the time. Not that that was any consolation to Benjamin, sitting at his mother's bedside, watching her struggle for life.

Two nurses in light blue scrubs had now politely asked him to leave the room briefly so they could check on his mother again. For the doctors and other medical staff, it was a continuous process. Still, few of them could hide their concerns for the woman who lay unconscious, hooked up to so many tubes most, with various beeping monitors.

One of the nurses asked Benjamin to follow her before going back to see his mother. She was taking him to speak with a doctor regarding his mother's condition. He walked alongside her, staring down at his feet as he followed the indication red line straight along the corridor. The other two colours, green and yellow, also there moments ago, had now disappeared down another corridor off to the left.

The nurse tapped gently on the office door and opened it without waiting for a reply. She informed the man sitting behind the small desk that she had brought Benjamin Cohen to see him. The doctor stood and offered his hand before indicating for him to sit. Benjamin hadn't made any eye contact as they shook hands. Instead, he was still inspecting his footwear.

"My name is Doctor Francis, Mr. Cohen. I don't know how much you understand regards your mother's condition. So, I'll try to make it as simple as possible. If that's okay with you?" Doctor Francis watched the young man's face. He seemed lost, bewildered. Close to tears. There were no words, just the slightest nod of the head.

"This must be hard for you as her nearest living relative, and I realise that. But we may have to make some very dramatic decisions in the next twenty-four hours. And I need you to be strong and ready. That's why I'm speaking with you now." Doctor Francis paused. He wasn't relishing the next few moments. In his experience, everyone handled the situation differently, and the young man sat looking down into his lap, looked close to losing it completely.

"Are you okay, Mr. Cohen? Would you like to do this a little later? Say, twenty minutes from now?" Doctor Francis had asked the questions, not even sure they had that much time. Benjamin looked up. His eyes were watery, and his cheeks were flushed.

"I'm fine. Carry on, doctor." He balled his fists together as he spoke nervously, tapping them against his chin. Doctor Francis sighed. He guessed that all hell was about to break loose, in some form or another. "Your mother is fortunate to be alive. She is a very strong woman. All that said, Mr. Cohen. Your mother has a broken pelvis, a double fracture of her left leg, plus a single fracture of her left arm. There is also some swelling around her brain. But it's her liver that is causing us the greatest concern. I'm afraid it is severely damaged."

Benjamin looked up properly for the first time. "So what can you do about it? You do know who my mother is, don't you?" His voice trembled ever so slightly but mentioning her name had made him straighten his back and widen his eyes. The doctor nodded that he understood the question. He sat back in his chair as he reflected on the young man's mother.

Marjorie Cohen was a pillar of the community. She donated thousands of dollars to just about every charity that contacted her. She was undoubtedly the wealthiest and most generous woman in the city, except where this hospital was concerned.

Doctor Francis had crossed swords with the woman only a few months ago when they both attended a prestigious black tie and ball gown dinner. The hospital was trying to raise money for a new surgical wing and all the specialised equipment required to run it successfully.

The eminent doctor and two of his fellow board members had approached Marjorie Cohen late in the evening. They and several others were doing the rounds, so to speak. Moving from one table to another, introducing themselves, checking that they had people's support. She was holding court across the other side of the room. Several prominent men and a few older ladies were hanging on her every word when they made their move.

Before Doctor Francis had even introduced his colleagues to her, he knew they were making a big mistake speaking with her now. She was intoxicated, swaying to and fro. Her words sounded slurred and incoherent. But by that time, they had committed themselves. This whole evening, the dinner, the live music was supposed to be about raising money for the new hospital wing.

No money from Marjorie Cohen was forthcoming. She had made that very clear. According to her, they needed to address their own running of the hospital first. Sort out some of the overpaid higher staff. *Try getting rid of the dead wood* had been her exact last words before turning back to those around her.

Doctor Francis smiled to himself as the three of them walked away from the embarrassing situation. He knew that it was probably his fault. He listened to his fellow board members as they tried to diagnose what had just happened. Why the reject? What was wrong with the woman? He knew only too well. He had once dated Marjorie Cohen. They had had dinner, and he had taken her home and refused the offer of a nightcap. Saying he had an early start in the morning but would call her later that week. He broke that promise, and they never saw each other again until today.

Now, she was lying in the hospital she had rejected just a few months ago. Needing their help to stay alive. Benjamin Cohen broke into his thoughts. "Doctor Francis. I asked if you knew who my mother was?" His voice sounded agitated at having to ask the question again. Doctor Francis raised a hand to acknowledge his silence.

"Yes, I know who your mother is, Benjamin. Our paths have crossed." He said no more. He could tell that the young man had something on his mind, and he had a fair idea of what was coming next. He also knew that his answer was going to be negative. Not what Benjamin wanted to hear.

"So, if you know who she is, you know that money is not a problem. How do we buy a new liver?" The doctor might have laughed if the situation wasn't quite so serious. "I'm afraid it's not as simple as that, Benjamin. There are lots of tests that we need to do. We would have to find a donor in the next forty-eight hours. Someone compatible with your mother…." Benjamin stood up abruptly, cutting the doctor off in mid-sentence. "Me." He said, prodding his chest several times. "I must be compatible. I'm her son." He was so proud of himself. It almost brought a smile to his pale face.

"That's possible, Benjamin, but there is no guarantee at this stage that you will be a match. Plus, you need to think this through carefully. Donating part of your liver is risky. We usually give counseling before as well as after."

"I want to be tested, no matter what the risks

are to me. This is my mother we're talking about. End of story."

"Well, doing blood and tissue tests are the first steps. After we have the results back, we'll speak again. In the meantime, I'll have a nurse show you to a cubicle." The doctor stood and offered his hand. For the first time since entering his office, Benjamin seemed so much more relaxed. His hand grip was certainly much firmer. His whole self-esteem was much more positive.

Having left Benjamin in the safe hands of a nurse, Doctor Francis hurried off to Marjorie Cohen's private room. He looked at the clipboard attached to the bottom of the bed. He was pleased with the results. There hadn't been any dramatic changes in her condition. He dropped the notes back into the metal holder and walked around to the side of the bed.

Marjorie's eyes were open. They looked vacant, as if she was focusing on nothing of importance. Doctor Francis leaned over so that she might recognise him. He looked down and smiled. "Hi, Marjorie. You sure are some hell of a fighter." His smile broadened as she closed her eyes as soon as she realised who he was.

"Just for the record, I didn't stand you up." He was nodding and wagging a friendly finger at her.

"You promised to call, and you didn't. It sure felt like I was being ignored. Stood up." Her voice was scratchy and croaky. She seemed in pain as she replied. He put a finger to his lips. "Ssshh. No talking right now. You need to rest. I'll see you shortly. I promise." He gave her a cheeky grin and walked away. Leaving Marjorie to listen to the constant hum and beep of the various monitors.

Alone in her private room, she had time to reflect on her life how she used her money and power to get everything she desired. The time in Venice when the shoe shop was just about to close. How she had bribed the young shop assistant with five hundred euros to stay open so she could try on the shoes that had taken her fancy in the window. They hadn't fitted. They were too tight, so she just left without as much as a thank you.

On the same vacation near Rome, she arranged, again with euros, for the manager of a restaurant to move a young couple because she had wanted to sit and eat outside at their table. Tears formed in her eyes as the memories flooded into her head. Was she really that insufferable? Yes, was the only reply she heard. It didn't sound nice, not one little bit.

Doctor Francis returned to the private room. A nurse was on observation duty. She was there to monitor everything. He stood over Marjorie and watched her sleep. Despite all the bruising around her face and the mess that her spikey white hair was in, she was still beautiful. He touched her hand lightly, carefully avoiding the pulse oximeter attached to her middle finger. His warmth was enough to make her open her eyes.

"Hi." He said, smiling down at her.

Hi." She replied, wanting to say more but not sure if she should.

"How you doing?" He inquired. That's a dumb question, he thought as soon as he had asked her. She tried to frown, but none of her facial muscles worked. He quickly realised what the problem was.

"It's okay to speak, but you must stop if it starts to feel uncomfortable."

"I think I'm doing okay." She replied, answering his question.

"Good. Listen. We've done some blood and tissue-type tests on your son Benjamin. I'm just waiting on the results. He's your best chance of us finding a match quickly enough." Marjorie began shaking her head.

"You already know that I have a rare blood type." The doctor nodded and leaned forward. Her voice was so quiet that he was struggling to hear her properly. "Robert. Can you ask the nurse to leave us and close the door behind her?" He stood up and turned around without questioning her request. "Nurse, we would like five minutes, please." She nodded and closed the door without being asked. His tone told her the severity of the situation.

Robert Francis pulled up a chair and sat as close as he could to Marjorie. He gently placed a hand on top of hers and waited. She took her time. He could tell that whatever she wanted to say wasn't going to be easy for her.

"Take your time Marjorie."

"Benjamin is not my son." Her eyes welled up, and tears ran down her cheeks. "Robert. Twenty-six years ago, I did something terrible. I was in hospital having a baby. There were complications, and the baby died within minutes of me giving birth. I was devastated, distraught. Out of my head, I was not thinking straight. A woman in the next bed to me, I think her name was Amanda, perhaps Miranda. God, I'm not even sure about that anymore. She was a single mother with no income and no way of supporting a child. I bought that child. I bought Benjamin from her." She stopped, almost struggling to breathe.

Doctor Francis leaned over the bed until their eyes met. "It's okay, Marjorie. I'm not here to judge you." He hadn't found that easy to say, but he needed to say something. The last thing he wanted was a hysterical patient on his hands. Already, he could see that her heart monitor had quickened.

"I'm not going to ask you to forgive me, Robert, but I will ask you not to tell Benjamin. He will probably find out one day, but not yet, please. Please, not now!" Doctor Francis stood and went to move the chair away.

"Robert, promise me you won't tell him?"

"I won't tell him, Marjorie. That's your job, Not mine." He cursed to himself as he walked away. He hadn't meant to sound that severe, but he had found that hard to accept. He turned back towards Marjorie. It was as if he needed to make amends for his inept comment.

"You need a liver, or partial liver transplant, Marjorie. Every possible avenue will be explored. We're here to save lives. That's what we do." He had just opened the door to leave when she spoke again.

"I saw a nurse dressed all in white. She stood at my bedside and spoke with me." Doctor Francis shook his head and returned to her bedside.

"No, that's not possible, Marjorie. Our nurses haven't worn white uniforms since the late 1980s."
"I saw her, Robert. She told me things. Things that I should do before you know what!"
"Marjorie, I can assure you that you didn't see a nurse

in a white uniform. They like me, wear these baggy blue scrubs. They're not the most attractive clothing, but they are the most practical and comfortable."

"She told me that I was going to die. That I had to follow a certain path before that happened." Marjorie paused. She didn't want to ask the next question. "I am going to die, aren't I, Robert?" Robert Francis was back at his patient bedside in an instant. He hesitated momentarily. He knew that he couldn't lie to this woman, but at the same time, he knew that telling her the truth would be very hard.

"We will and are doing everything humanly possible." He looked away at the monitors behind the bed. Marjorie was too wise not to see that.

"You're not a very good liar, doctor Francis. I know when I'm beaten, and so should you. I would like to see Benjamin now." He nodded, but he was also embarrassed. She had read him like a book and knew the ending before it had even been written.

Twelve Months Later.

There was a lot of pomp and ceremony within the hospital walls. Outside, the traffic had either been stopped or diverted. The male members of the hospital board wore black suits and bow ties. The nurses were all dressed in special white uniforms for the occasion. There weren't any blue scrubs to be seen.

Benjamin Cohen was the focal point. He stood smiling, his hand gripping the braided cord that was attached to the small gold curtain. He gave it a gentle tug, and everyone present applauded as the new shiny plaque was revealed. He smiled with pride when he read. THE BENJAMIN COHEN WING Opened on

20th August 2022. Thanks to the kind generosity of the late Marjorie Cohen.

AMONG THE BRAMBLES

Inspired by: LIVE FOREVER.
Performed by OASIS

I had been here many times before, standing and staring over the old wooden five-bar gate, as if I was waiting for something magical to happen, that the old house was suddenly going to materialise before my very eyes. Even though I'm not that much of a daydreamer, this place and allotments draw me here two or three times a month. Thanks mainly to the family journals handed down, which seem to have drawn me into our family past.

These allotments still bear the name of where my great grandparents used to live, Oak Lodge. Several years ago, the big house that once stood here was torn down as an unsafe building. Evidently, it had been built on soft sandy ground, and when the Basingstoke canal was constructed at the rear of the house, it may have contributed to the foundation's problem.

The land was vacant for many years until a developer who thought he knew better purchased the overgrown three acres with the bright idea of building a complex of modern-day houses, which was the last thing the nearby residents wanted. Fortunately for everyone concerned, he went bust before any building work had started.

The local council then stepped in and purchased it from the builder. They listened to the locals and turned the site into allotments. That was back in nineteen forty-five, when the second world war had just finished, and food was in short supply. Soldiers were returning from war-torn lands and were encouraged to rent a plot and grow their own food.

Now, seventy-seven years later, in twenty-twenty-two, I have my very own plot, the exact one I have yearned for. I had waited patiently, turning down several offers of other plots here, plus at additional locations throughout the town. I wanted the one I now have for a very good reason. That is, of course, if my grandparents are to be believed.

This is what I know. My great grandfather left his wife Alice and three children and sailed to America in the winter of 1890. He went, assuring his family that he had the promise of a great job and would send for his wife and children once he was settled. They never heard from him again, and it wasn't long before my great-grandmother had to leave her home. By all accounts, it was a big house with five bedrooms, two main lounges, a back room, and a big kitchen.

There are stories, not in the journals, that Archibald, my great grandfather, was a handsome man. He was also a bit of a womaniser. There are tales of him having several affairs during his marriage to my great-grandmother.

It seems that he also gambled heavily, cards mainly, I believe, but whatever his addiction was, it eventually cost him his job in Woking, where he had worked all his life in banking. Hence his desire to start a new life in another country.

All of this happened shortly after his elderly mother died. Her death certificate states the cause of death as heart failure. The story goes that she was eating her Sunday dinner with my great-grandparents and suddenly began choking. She clutched her chest and tried to stand up but collapsed to the floor and died.

She was a very remarkable lady. She had insisted that she wanted to be cremated. That doesn't mean much in this day and age, but when I checked back through the records, I found that, in Woking, where, as it happened, the first ever cremation took place back in 1887. By 1888, only twenty-five other cremations had taken place, so she was one of those.

My great-grandfather was devastated. He sat around the house during the day, made no attempt to look for work, and at night went out, getting up to who knows what. It broke my great-grandmother's heart, and according to the journals I've read, it caused her to have a breakdown of some kind. Other family members looked after her, so there were no doctors involved.

It was three months before things started getting back to normal. If trying to bring up three young children without any money coming in is normal. Alice certainly seems to have managed quite well. They sold a few items of furniture, some family heirlooms, and kept their heads above water without anything changing in the household. My great grandfather still didn't have a job and ventured out several nights a week.

During my research, I discovered that the local paper ran an article about a mysterious punter winning a large amount of money at Royal Ascot in 1890. A horse fittingly named Gold won the Gold Cup that year. In one of the journals, it was interesting that my great-grandmother mentioned that *"Archie came home last night and produced three gold sovereigns from his waistcoat pocket. I cried. We suddenly had money, not much, be we had some."* That was the winter he left for America.

So, this is my first day down at the allotments. I was feeling excited. I was pushing my wheelbarrow like a man possessed. I was weaving one way to dodge a woman walking her dog and then bouncing down the gutter and into the main road to avoid two joggers, who were so busy chatting that they didn't see me until the last second. My spade, fork, and long handles secateurs were jumping all over the place even though I'd thought to put a stretch bungy over them all for security on the short journey.

A smiling elderly gentleman opened the gate as I arrived. "You look enthusiastic!" he said, closing it as soon as I was on the grassy path.

"Sure am. It's my first day here." I replied, catching my breath. He was already nodding back at me. "I could tell by the speed you came down the road." We both smiled pleasantries. I knew he was right. I had hardly slept a wink last night.

"So which plot have you got then?" He asked, looking around the various allotments. I pointed over to the far corner where the big oak tree dominated. It was tucked right up between where the two original walls met.

"Oh, you don't want that plot. Nothing will grow there. That bloody tree will see to that. We've been protesting about it for years. It sucks everything out of the ground. All the water, all the nutrients, and gives nothing back, except shade, of course, and we don't want that, do we?"

"I'll be okay," I replied, raising the barrow's handles, hoping to move on.

"There's a plot next to mine going. The ground is good. The last tenant, old Bill, looked after it. He put loads of fertilizer down. Horse manure, you name it, he used it."

"I'm fine, thanks." Without waiting for a response, I wheeled my way along the grass path and headed for my plot. The plot I wanted. The one I had waited for so patiently. I was aware that I was being followed. My smiling gatekeeper was trundling along behind me. I refused to look back as I tried to rehearse what to say to him when I arrived without being rude. I just wanted to get on with the work at hand, nothing more.

"Look at all them bloody brambles!" He said the moment I came to a halt. "No one since I've been here has accepted this plot. It's too overgrown. Bloody Semtex wouldn't sort that lot out." He gestured an explosive reaction with his arms before pointing an accusing finger in the main direction of my plot of land. I stood silently looking. The area was smothered in impenetrable spiky thick, tangled brambles.

I could see what he meant, but I already knew all that. I had sneaked in here often, usually late evening when no one else was around. I even have at least a dozen, maybe more, pictures of this plot on my phone, not that I was about to reveal that to the gatekeeper. "I'll manage," I replied, turning to face him and giving him our family trait, death stare. It worked. It usually did. He shrugged, turned away, and left me to my own devices.

I pulled the rucksack off my back and dropped it to the floor, where I slowly set about undoing the top strap, using it as a ploy to watch my unwanted guest. He seemed in no rush as he strolled back along the grassy footpath to his own allotment. He was constantly shaking his head in disbelief while probably muttering to himself, what an idiot I was.

I worked for a solid hour. Only stopping twice for a welcoming drink of water and several bites from one of the two bananas that I had remembered to bring with me. It was a challenging, tiring task, made more difficult by the audience I now had. Three other allotment holders were standing watching with the gatekeeper, who was no doubt filling them in on just how much of a stupid and stubborn person I seemed to be.

They didn't realise that I knew exactly what I was doing. Well, almost. I certainly will when I find what I'm looking for. Which I felt sure wouldn't be long now. If one of the other plot holders had come and introduced themselves to me, it wouldn't look like I had achieved very much. I had cut and dragged brambles and undergrowth from different areas, making it look very haphazard. While all the time, I was checking the site for the layer of bricks that I knew had once been there.

The journals back home had talked of a small hut, come potting shed. Near the big oak tree, that's what I was looking for, foundation bricks. That was my only interest. I mean, I'm twenty-eight years of age. I'm not into gardening and growing things.

I had to borrow all of this stuff from my neighbour Colin. His front and back gardens are immaculate. They look like something you would see in a posh magazine. He even had to show me how to use the secateurs.

"Don't try cutting down branches that are too thick." He had warned me three times before he had even handed them over. I'm sure he didn't believe me when I told him I was helping one of my mates clear his elderly grandfather's garden. That said, he gave me two pairs of thick cotton protective gloves, saying he didn't need them back.

I was done for the day. I should have been pleased with my work. I had a large heap of brambles, what seemed like half a ton of assorted weeds and nettles, and a severe back ache. What I didn't have was any bricks, not a single one. I needed a hot shower and a revisit to the journals. I was missing something. Something important.

I was halfway down my second bottle of beer halfway through the second journal when I saw it. *"A.B. Archie has cut another branch from the great oak. It caught on the roof of his potting shed and really annoyed him."* There it was, the information that I wanted. I couldn't recall ever reading that before. Perhaps I had, but it just didn't register. It did cast a little doubt in my mind, though. Where had I read about the bricks that supposedly supported the potting shed? Tomorrow, I tackle the brambles beneath the great oak, then we'll see.

The gatekeeper wasn't there when I arrived, for which I was genuinely grateful. The shock I did get when I walked to my plot was that all the weeds and brambles had gone. I looked around the allotment in disbelief, and then I saw in the opposite corner the massive compost heaps. I walked over quickly, I had more pressing matters to attend to, but I wanted to see for myself. Sure enough, there were my brambles. All cut up smaller and stacked in a great pile. The nettles and weeds were there as well, in a different heap.

"You need to tidy up as you go along." Someone said, walking towards me. It wasn't the gatekeeper. This chap had a walking stick and looked very unsteady on his feet. "It's in the rules, young man. You best read them if you want to stay on this site." I was lost for words. Who was he, the president or something? He half smiled at me as he stretched his out. "I'm the president of the allotment society. Walter Groves." I shook his hand firmly, even though I was feeling confused. Where had he just sprung from? There was no one here when I arrived. "Steve Bowman," I said, our hands still locked together. The half-smile turned into a huge grin.

"You're not related to the Bowman family that used to live here, are you?" He knew the answer before I had even opened my mouth to tell him. "You are. I can see the likeness now. Well, well, well. Wait till I tell my missus. Her mother used to be a maid for the Bowmans. We still live in the little cottage back there, by the canal." He waved his stick towards a thicket of trees. I released his hand, and half turned. I couldn't see a cottage, but I knew the canal was in that direction.

I watched Walter hobble away. I was still

curious to see how he had managed to get here so quickly, undetected. Then I saw the answer. There was a small wrought iron gate in the far wall, which he closed with his stick once on the other side. After that, he disappeared into the trees and was gone from sight.

He had taken the trouble to explain that the other members still tending their allotments had cleared up after me and suggested that I thank them profusely when I next see them. Except for the guy I keep calling the gatekeeper, who I know now is called Ron, I wouldn't have a clue whose name matches which face.

I was eager to get on. I looked around the allotment and was still the only person. Perhaps, the threat of rain was keeping everyone away? Walter had assured me that it was going to rain until late tonight. That had cheered me up no end. I can have a whole day here if need be. I've even brought sandwiches this time.

By lunch, working under a cloudy rain-threatening sky, I had cleared enough of the brambles to reveal my first row of bricks excitedly. The oak tree had done its job. It had slowed the growth of everything down. Ron, the gatekeeper, knows his stuff. I didn't stop to eat. I carried on hacking away at the brambles, desperately trying to find the final row.

Lunch was served. A bottle of lukewarm water, plus two rounds of cheese and lettuce sandwiches, with enough salad cream to sink a battleship. I pulled the journal out of my rucksack and sat beneath the oak tree. For whatever reason, I felt that the book should be here with me if I was going to find what I was expecting. I opened up the first marked page and read what I assumed Alice had written aloud. *"I have buried his mother's ashes behind the potting shed. They were bothering me sat there on his writing bureau. A constant reminder of how things were once upon a time."* The second page read, again, I assumed by Alice. *"I don't think Archie will be sending for us from America. I haven't told the kids. They're too young to understand. I will wait and see what happens."*

I'm not sure why finding the urn with my great great grandmother's ashes is so important to me. It just feels like the right thing to do. It's part of our family history just because my great grandfather left his wife and abandoned his children. Doesn't change the fact that it's a part of me. It's a part of my life. Something that I need to understand. My mother always believed that Archibald left for America with one of his lady friends, whom she so politely called them. That's life. That's what happens sometimes. No matter how hard it must have been for my great-grandmother to accept, she got on with her life and made the most of a bad situation.

Once the journal was safely tucked back in my bag, I began gently digging, probing the ground around the base outline of the bricks. I started closest to the tree. The ground was pretty soft, and within minutes, the fork I was using juddered against something. I immediately thought that I'd hit a tree root. I changed to the spade and gently dug around the area. I needed a trowel, but the spade would have to do it.

It turned out not to be part of the oak tree's root system but what looked like one of those old-fashioned tea caddies I had seen on The Antique

Roadshow or some programme. I made enough room around the container to place both my hands beneath it, and then I eased it carefully out of the ground, where it had been buried, I assumed, for the past two hundred and thirty-odd years.

Just as I was about to stand up, staring wonderfully at my find, the bottom gave way and dropped back into the small pit I had just dug. Fine grey dust drifted away on the air. Other particles fell around my feet, leaving me holding an empty casket. I felt utterly devastated. My great great grandmother's ashes had been there all this time, and now I had helped cast them to the wind, losing them forever.

I looked down even though I knew that there wouldn't be enough of the ash to retrieve. It was already blowing across the bricks and my allotment. I knelt in front of the freshly dug hole. I felt that I should say something, even if it were only goodbye. It was then that I saw the first shiny coin. I went to pick it up and saw another one, and then another.

I now had twenty gold sovereigns. Greedily, I picked up the spade and started digging a little deeper. Perhaps there were more? I saw something beneath the surface, but it wasn't gold. It looked white. I cast the spade to one side and began digging with both my hands. I fell backwards in horror when I saw the curvature of the human skull and the two big empty eye sockets staring up at me.

Once I had regained my composure, I called the police. I told them what I had discovered. Well, not all you understand. They told me to stay there and not to touch anything. I assured them I wouldn't. The sovereigns were already in my rucksack. I wouldn't need to touch them until I got home.

FOREVER LOYAL

Inspired by: I WILL ALWAYS LOVE YOU.
Performed by WHITNEY HOUSTON

"No, no, no. I cannot allow anyone to have a dog in this nursing home. And that's final." Anthony Walker sat behind his desk and massaged his forehead gently. This was the second time in two weeks that one of the nurses had asked the same question. He flinched at the sound of his office door being closed. *"Whatever next?"* He said quietly under his breath. *"Please may my mother bring Miss Pickles, her cat? And can mine bring her two budgerigars, Boo Boo and Yogi?"* He almost smiled as the bird's two names popped into his head. His two young children had been watching cartoons as he left the house for work this morning. He guessed he knew which ones they were.

Anthony Walker needed to address this problem once and for all. Alison Goodge was a damn fine nurse, but when she got a bee in her bonnet like now, she never knew when enough was enough. He decided to speak with Karen Cross, the Matron at Sea View Court. She had been here even longer than he had, and she certainly understood her nurses better than he did. At the moment, Alison Goodge was rocking the boat, and he didn't need that kind of pressure.

"Thanks for coming on your break." He said, inviting Karen to sit and pushing a coaster across his desk for her mug of coffee. She took a quick sip and placed it down.

"What's the problem?" She asked, giving him a knowing smile. He pursed his lips together. "Who said there was a problem?"

"Tony, I've seen that expression on your face so many times over the years. I know you have a problem." He sat back and clasped his hands behind his head.

"You're too bright by half, Matron." He replied, swivelling in his chair gently. Karen glanced at her watch and rescued her coffee from the desk.

Anthony Walker saw the concerned frown and sat forward. "Sorry, Karen, I'll get on with it. Alison has been to see me twice in the past ten days." He saw Karen smile. The look on her face told him that she knew what was coming, she was never able to control her expressions.

"Okay, you know. So, tell me what the word is out there?" He waved his hand towards his office door.

"The word out there is. That Graham Kelly has recently lost his wife suddenly to cancer. He has been admitted to us with severe dementia because there is now no family member to look after him, and we have insisted that his Bitza dog, Netty, be placed in kennels."

"Netty the Bitza! What sort of dog is a Bitza?" Karen was going to enjoy this. She knew how little her boss liked animals. "A Bitza is a multi-mixed breed dog." She replied, leaving her answer short on purpose. She wanted the opportunity to emphasise her punchline. She knew the dog situation was causing some friction with her staff. Some, like Alison, felt strongly about the dog being allowed to stay with its master. Regardless of how inconvenient or practical it was.

Anthony Walker submitted. He raised both of his hands, showing her his palms. "Right, you win. I have no idea what is coming next. But I sure as hell know that you do. Let's have it. Both barrels, I suspect."

"A Bitza dog is a dog made up from bits of this and bits of that." Even though Anthony shook his head and pulled a disgruntled face at her, she laughed loudly.

"Okay, trying to make light of the situation always was your style. But Alison is causing me a headache, a bloody big one. I think that you need to speak with her. Explain that when I say no, I mean no. We can't have a dog running around the nursing home, yapping and barking, doing whoopsies everywhere." Karen nearly choked on the coffee she had just sipped into her mouth.

"Whoopsies!" She exclaimed, her eyes wide in astonishment, as she wiped a dribble of the warm liquid from her chin. Anthony shrugged. "What's wrong with whoopsies? That's what dogs do, don't they?"

"Yes, Tony. That's what dogs do. I'll speak with Alison at lunchtime. Is that all?" She pushed the chair back and stood up. Anthony nodded, and she headed towards the office door. "Whoopsies." She muttered under her breath and shook her head before closing it behind her.

When Karen arrived in the main lounge, there seemed to be a lot of confusion going on. One of her nurses, Tracey, was speaking quietly with a new care assistant who appeared to be very close to tears. Karen moved them away to the far corner of the room.

"What's going on? Is everything alright?" She asked the question knowing full well that there was a problem of some kind.

"I assigned Rose to sit with Mr. Kelly. She went to make him a cup of tea, and now we don't know where he is." Even the nurse's voice was breaking up at the severity of the problem. Karen stayed calm, at least on the outside. "You've done all the obvious things? Checked his room? Checked the toilet? Spoken with reception?"

"Haven't been to the reception yet, but his room is empty, and so is the toilet on this floor." The nurse sounded more confident now, but the care assistant was visibly shaking. Karen rested her hand on her arm. "It's okay, Rose. He can't be very far away. You go and check upstairs. Tracey, you come with me to reception." They went their separate ways, with Karen and Tracey walking briskly towards the main doors.

"I'm ever so sorry, Matron. I was called away to the kitchen. The chef had a dietary problem he wanted to discuss with me regarding Mrs. Montgomery, the lady who arrived yesterday." They were walking so quickly that Tracey was out of breath. Karen dismissed her excuses with a wave of her hand. All of that could and would be sorted out later on when Graham Kelly had been located.

"Claire, have you seen Mr. Kelly recently?" Claire tapped her screen and then swiped her finger across it several times. She was bringing up photographs of all the current residents. She looked up and smiled. "He stepped outside about ten minutes ago." She informed Matron, nodding at the photo and looking up from the computer screen.

Karen Cross was just about to protest at the idea that anyone should be allowed to step outside, as her receptionist had so nicely put it when Claire turned the day book around for her to read it. "Alison signed out with him at 13:10. She said she was on her lunch break and would be back before two." Claire gave Matron her customary sweet smile and returned to her duties.

Karen read the book for herself. Next to Alison's signature was the word social therapy. She now knew precisely where the pair of them had gone. Karen checked her watch. They were due back in forty-five minutes. She decided by the time she had driven to The K9 Sanctuary. They would be making their way back, and she knew she had to be here when they returned.

After telling Tracey to go and find Rose and tell her the news, Karen began pacing up and down the reception area. Checking her watch every few minutes wasn't helping her stress levels. She was like a ticking time bomb, her anger pumping harder and harder through her body. She dismissed one of the carers who had been sent to find her. The poor girl was supposed to inform her that lunch was ready. Instead, she was sent away without any explanation.

She saw the taxi pull up outside and watched as Alison helped Graham Kelly shuffle out of the vehicle. "Claire, will you please call Tracey to reception and then ask her to take charge of Mr. Kelly? Thank you." Without waiting for a reply, she headed for the main door. She was shaking her head and had her sternest disapproving face on. Alison closed her eyes when she saw Matron approaching.

"Graham," She began, taking his arm and leading towards the door. "how was the trip to see Netty? Was Netty pleased to see you?" Karen emphasised the dog's name. Graham's dementia was severe enough that she was still to hear him speak more than three words.

"Netty, good." His face lit up as a broad happy smile spread across it. Karen immediately glanced across to Alison. She had tears welling up in her eyes. "It was absolutely amazing." She began to say. But her Matron was already stopping her.

"Not now, Alison. And please wait here until I return." Karen slowly walked Graham Kelly into reception. Tracey arrived on cue and took over.

"Where have you been, Graham? We were all worried about you." She said, escorting him along the corridor, knowing that she wouldn't receive a reply. Karen turned on her heels as soon as Graham Kelly was in safe hands and headed back outside. She pointed a finger and told Alison they should walk away from the building.

"What the hell were you thinking?" Before Alison could respond, Karen was back on the attack. "All the staff has heard about your little antics, so it won't be long before Anthony hears about your stupid exploits. And then the S.H. one T. will really hit the fan." They stopped walking and stood beneath the big wooden pergola. It was the one blind spot in the beautifully landscaped garden and a favourite place for staff and family members to talk privately.

"He was pining for Netty. I know he was… You should have seen his face when she ran to him, and they greeted each other. It was so wonderful to see."

"But you were told. Only this morning, you broached the subject with Anthony Walker. Why go straight to the Director? There are procedures. Correct ways of doing things, and bulldozing isn't one of them."

"I had to do something, Matron. He was feeling and acting miserable. Ask any of the other nurses. They will tell you the same. I would do it again in a heartbeat."

"You might not get the chance, my girl. What you have just done isn't ethical, for starters. What if something had happened to the poor man? Where would we be then?" Alison hung her head.

At last, reality had finally dawned on her. Karen looked out across the Bristol Channel. She wanted to give her nurse time to compose herself. Sea View Court was aptly named. The purpose-built building sat perched high on the cliffs along the main coast road, and Karen could see parts of Wales on sunny days like today.

Karen turned back to her nurse. "You are a damn good nurse, but your emotions sometimes get the better of you. As it happens, Mr. Walker left the premises before you did, but not before he had informed me about your meeting with him. He isn't going to be pleased, Alison."

"I know, and I'm sorry, Matron."

"You are not Wonder Woman and certainly

not the Lone Ranger, and neither Mr. Walker nor I, for that matter, wish to be Tonto. Do I make myself clear?" Alison nodded, and Matron indicated that the discussion was over. They both walked back through the grounds in silence.

Anthony Walker indicated for Karen to take a seat. He then contacted reception. "Claire, will you page Alison Goodge and ask her to come along to my office immediately? Thank you." He looked up at Karen. She gave him a reassuring smile. She knew that he wasn't a hundred percent convinced that they were doing the right thing.

Claire had been at Sea View Court long enough not to announce to the whole building that the Director wanted to see the nurse in his office. "Will nurse Alison please come along to reception? Nurse Alison to reception, please." She felt a pang of remorse for having to be the one to inform Alison what was going on.

When she arrived at the reception area, several nurses were already there waiting to give her some support. Everyone knew the situation. Yes, she had overstepped the mark, but her heart was in the right place. She was one of the most caring nurses in the specialist unit.

Tracey gave her a big hug. While Rose, the young care assistant, stood quietly, almost in tears. Other staff members patted her gently on the back and offered words of encouragement. She knew that everyone was behind her.

It was a long walk along the thickly carpeted corridor. One of the nurses, popped her head out of a patient's room. "Good luck Ali." Alison nodded her appreciation and turned the corner to face the Director's office. She took a deep breath. She knew that the future of her whole career lay waiting in that room.

She tapped nervously on the door and waited. "Come." She shuddered at the sound of his tone. Anthony Walker had a deep gruff voice, and even when he was being pleasant, he always sounded slightly grumpy. Alison entered his office and was pleased to see Matron sitting on the other side of his desk.

"Please sit, Alison." He nodded at the vacant chair, which seemed purposely set aside for her. She sat and placed her hands on her lap. She intended to act as calmly as possible, but inside, her stomach seemed to be enjoying the full benefits of a trampoline.

"Alison, where do I start? Have you any idea of the repercussions of your actions the other day?" Anthony sat back, giving her time to think through her response. She began nodding and pursed her lips together. He felt that she was holding back. "This is the time for you to speak up. I know Matron has spoken with you, but I'm interested in what you have to say."

Alison cleared her throat. It felt dry and restricted, and she needed to put her case clearly and firmly. She believed in what she had done, even though she thought it was about to cost her her job.

"Graham Kelly came to us shortly after losing his wife. She was also his carer, and he relied on her for everything. Netty was also a considerable part of his life. His dementia inhibits his speech, but Netty is the one word I have often heard. He struggles to say it, but he always perseveres until he gets it right. Netty is enormously important in his life, and I believe they are both pining for each other differently."

Alison glanced across to her Matron, hoping for some sign that she hadn't said too much. Karen sat looking straight ahead, showing no emotion at all. Alison sighed. She was hoping for more. Just a little nod of the head would have been excellent.

"But that doesn't excuse your actions. Taking a patient on a road trip without consulting with anyone beforehand was completely reckless." He paused to give himself time to consider his following words. "Matron and I have spoken at length regarding your conduct. And while I have slight reservations, I trust the fact that Matron knows her nursing staff better than I do. It's called teamwork, Alison. It's how the system works. So, accept this as a verbal warning. It will not go on your records, and Matron will tell you why." He looked over to Karen Cross, who leaned forward and smiled at Alison for the first time since she had entered the room.

"Wendy Riley has had a private word with me. As you probably know, she has been on an IVF programme for some time, and finally, she has a happy result. She has confirmed that she is pregnant." Alison couldn't contain her pleasure. Sister Wendy had been trying for about five years, and now her dream had come true.

"That's wonderful news. I'm so thrilled for her." Alison was beaming with joy for her colleague.

"She hasn't told anyone else yet, but from her happy smiling face, I'm guessing it won't be long before one of the other nurses puts two and two together. So, why tell you when the others don't yet know? Well, Wendy recommended you for her job. I think you are the ideal person to step into that role, regardless of your trip out." Karen looked straight at Alison. "Over to you."

"What can I say?" She began.

"Yes, I accept. Thank you, would be a good start." Matron was now grinning at her. Karen suddenly realised the magnitude of what had just been proposed to her.

"Yes, I accept. Thank you." She paraphrased back. No longer able to withhold her emotions, tears formed in her eyes.

"Good, that's settled then." Anthony Walker interrupted and broke the silence in the room. Alison stood up to leave.

"Before you go, there's one more thing. Thanks to you, my family has a new addition. After you came to see me, I spoke with my extremely understanding wife, Elizabeth. She and our six-year-old twins then went to The K9 Sanctuary. It seems that they fell in love with a dog called Netty. Who I'm led to believe will soon be making daily visits to Sea View Court. So, thank you, Sister Alison, soon to be. I'm sure I'll eventually get used to going home and finding a dog asleep in my favourite armchair."

Alison could hardly control her feelings. The tears that were in her eyes moments ago were now streaming down her face. She went to speak. She felt that she needed to say thank you at the very least. Anthony saw the look on her face and put his hand up.

"Go. Save your thoughts for another day. Perhaps when I've become used to having a dog around, you can say I told you so. In the meantime, do your new job with the same passion you are showing now." He smiled before adding. "But Alison, please try and stay within the guidelines."

LAST CHANCE SALOON

Inspired by: HEARTBREAK HOTEL.
Performed By ELVIS PRESLEY

I was here under false pretences. I was kidding myself that coming to this convention would enhance my chances of having a normal relationship. It had all sounded so easy, so wonderful. *"We will help you. We will support you. We will find you your perfect partner."* What the advertising campaign failed to say was. *"Or your money back."* That's what the small print should have said. *"If we can't find the love of your life, we won't take a penny."* No chance of that happening, and no chance of me getting a £500 refund.

However, the manor house hosting the event did look pretty spectacular as I drove up the long, gravelled driveway. Perhaps I was judging this weekend too soon after all. Keep an open mind, David. You might be pleasantly surprised. There I go again, trying to nuzzle down into my comfort zone where everything feels safe and at ease with the world.

Registration was 11:30 a.m. And I was very early. My Sat Nav had informed me that my journey into the heart of rural Buckinghamshire would take just over two hours. It took me an hour and three-quarters, and I wasn't speeding. No one on this planet can speed in a Fiat 500. Except perhaps my mother, of course, when she borrowed it for the day last month, she bragged that she clocked ninety-five miles an hour.

Concerned about a mechanical problem, I took it to the local garage. The nice friendly man there said that the speedometer wasn't faulty and that I wasn't to worry. Well, I do. My little Pricilla isn't used to being thrashed along the highways and bye-ways of England. Sixty-five miles an hour is plenty fast enough for her.

I walked up the steps to the main door, stopping to admire the two large stone lions that sat on either side. They were so majestic, sitting there guarding the place, keeping us all safe.

The lovely lady at reception informed me that my room wasn't ready yet, and advised me to take a stroll around the grounds and return in half an hour. That was over an hour ago, and I'm perturbed. I can't see the manor house from here. There are so many trees in the way. Moreover, the narrow path I was on has now completely disappeared.

"Help. Is there anyone about?" I shouted so loudly I thought my lungs were going to explode. I looked in every direction. I had turned around so many times now that I couldn't remember which way I had been facing. "Help someone. I need help." My heart was racing, and my stomach was churning over. I was in the middle of nowhere, with no map, compass, torch, or anything of use. I'd left my mobile in the car.

"This is serious," I shouted. "I'm lost and about to die. Someone, help me, please."

"Cooee. Over here." I turned a complete

circle but still couldn't see anyone.

"To your right. I'm over here...No, not that hand. Hold up your other one. Good, now look through your fingers. There I am, waving back at you." I ran towards the soft, comforting female voice. I tripped on a small branch hidden in the thick undergrowth but was up in a flash, legging it towards her.

Several other people were also sitting at the picnic tables when I arrived, all tousled and messy. A man looked up from his mobile, shook his head, and went straight back to double thumbing his text message. Clever sod, I thought before looking to thank the lady that had saved me.

"Thank you so much." I smiled. "I was completely lost there for a minute." I heard the thumb texter snigger behind me, but I ignored him because right now, I was mesmerised by the most beautiful electric blue eyes I had ever seen. That said, I did suppose that the thick lenses of her glasses probably magnified them somewhat.

"I'm Dorothy. My friends call me Dotty. Actually, it's just Mary that calls me Dotty. I guess she's the only friend I really have." She pursed her lips and looked down at the ground. All embarrassed that she only had one friend. I wish I knew Mary. She might also agree to become my friend as well, and then Dorothy and I could share her.

"What were you doing in the woods?" Dorothy asked me as she seemed to regain her confidence. It was now my turn to feel awkward. "Oh," I hunched my shoulders as I tended to do when I was about to tell a lie. "I was looking for the lesser spotted woodpecker," I told her confidently.

Dorothy smiled and shook her head, her long auburn hair flicking from side to side.

"You would be very fortunate to see a lesser spotted woodpecker around here. They are almost extinct in England. Plenty in Europe and even Japan. Besides that, they are such a tiny bird to spot, not much bigger than a sparrow." I gave her a knowing nod of my head. "Yes, of course they are," I added, still looking straight into her blue eyes.

"I was about to head back to the manor. I don't suppose you fancy walking with me, do you?" I was already nodding and smiling. Dorothy set off, and I followed two or three paces behind her.

"David, you can walk with me. I won't bite you." I skipped quickly to catch her up. I was desperate to make some conversation. But every thought that popped into my head swiftly erased itself before I could even put the sentence together. No wonder Amanda left me, calling me a geek and a waste of space.

I loved Amanda. She was beautiful, funny, and very intelligent. Intelligent enough to leave me, I guess. We had six weeks of bliss together. We went out to a restaurant once and to the cinema once. She had to pay on both occasions. I had just lost my job at the local gym. My profile didn't fit in very well with all those keep-fit fanatics. The person who hired me was working her notice. It was her last day there. I think she took pity on me or did it out of revenge.

"David!" I looked across at Dorothy. "I've asked you twice now. Are you here for The Mending of Hearts Weekend?"

"Yes, I am. Sorry. I was reminiscing. I was miles away. Sorry again." I sounded and felt all flustered. She had caught me thinking about Amanda. I needed to try and forget about her and concentrate on the here and now. This weekend was supposed to change my life as well as my bank balance. £500, what was I thinking?

"Oh, that's so nice when someone goes out of their way to find true love. Good luck then."

"Thank you. I think I'm going to need it."

"Here we are, then." Dorothy stopped, and I looked to see where we were. I hadn't noticed anything on our short walk together. "You need to go around to the front of the building." She said and pointed towards a narrow gravel path.

"Aren't you coming with me?" I asked, trying not to sound disappointed.

"Oh, gosh, no. I work here. Bye, David." She smiled, and before I could respond, she had walked to the back door and vanished from sight. I stuffed my hands deep into my trouser pockets and strolled around the building.

By ten to one, I had showered, changed into my smarter ripped jeans, and was looking forward to my lunch. I hesitated outside the dining room. I needed time to allow my stomach to stop rising and falling in anticipation of who might be in there waiting for me. I walked through the open door. No one, not a single soul.

"Excuse me, sir. "I turned to face a young lady wearing a black pencil skirt. I always look at the legs first. She also wore a white blouse under a black waistcoat and a red silk scarf around her neck. "Lunch is being served in the breakfast room." She indicated that she would guide me there.

"Lunch in the breakfast room. What's all that about?" I asked myself as I followed Miss Legs the short distance across the hallway to another room.

"There we are, sir." She stretched her arm out towards the open door.

"Thank you," I replied, but I could already hear the sound of flat-soled shoes slapping on the tiled floor. She was back to her busy schedule.

I ate my lunch of prawns and avocado salad in silence. People that entered after me chose to sit somewhere different. I had one of the eight big round tables all to myself. At least this wasn't the get-together, Although, from all the chatter, I could hear most of them were already getting to know each other. I scanned the room eagerly, and there were at least five Amandas for me to get to know.

The get-together was really awkward for me. It seems that there are seventeen of us. Seventeen lonely lost souls with stories to tell. It's a shame that no one heard mine. I slipped out of the room to use the bathroom. When I returned, everyone else had been paired up. They were taking turns speaking and listening to their respective partners. I spent most of the session twittering about Amanda to Francesca, the young lady in charge. She sometimes looked so bored, checking her fingernails before licking her index finger and smoothing down her perfectly formed eyebrows. I wasn't sure when to stop. Evidently, she did. "David, shall I walk you along and introduce you to Penny? She's our Specialist Healer, and she is absolutely fantastic. You can be the first to meet her. She uses different stones to help release emotions or spiritual blocks."

I followed Francesca through a labyrinth of different corridors. There were so many twists and turns that I was half expecting to be back where we started. Francesca tapped lightly on the door, just below the sign that read, Penny. Specialist Healer. We were in the right place then. I may need a map for the return journey.

Francesca mouthed something too quietly to Penny for me to hear. She was probably letting her know that I was a non-believer. I knew I shouldn't have kept mumbling about, *"how will a few stones mend a broken heart?"* to myself as I hurried along behind my guide.

"Penny, this is David. I'm sure you can work your wonders on him. He's been through a lot, poor soul." How does she know that? She's hardly said more than half a dozen words to me. In that case, I guess she has done me the courtesy of reading my CV, or whatever it was called. I did go on a bit about Amanda. She may have left me, but her presence still seems to be everywhere.

I slipped my shoes and socks off and clambered on the massage table. I lay face up on Penny's instructions and focused on a tiny crack in the ceiling that caught my eye. And then I waited in anticipation.

"Just try and relax, David. I can sense how nervous you are. This isn't going to hurt. In fact, it should be the complete opposite." Doesn't she know I have a weak back? How heavy are these stones going to be anyway?"

Madame Lydia Fortune Teller Extraordinaire, the door sign read. This was turning into a circus come carnival. Really! Did I sign up to go and see a fortune teller? I turned to go. There was no way I was knocking on that door.

"Please come in and take a seat." Her voice stopped me in my tracks. The door was closed, so how did she know I was hovering outside? Silly me. Of course, she knew I was there. She's a clairvoyant, after all. I checked around the edge of the door frame. I was looking for a camera, but I found nothing, so now intrigue was gripping me and pushing me through the door.

"Sit. Please sit while I close my eyes and tune myself into your persona." I was nearly wetting myself. Madame Lydia was dressed in a full-length flowery skirt and matching blouse. On her head, she wore a tight-fitting scarf covered in gold discs. But I found the silky, vibrant coloured mask beneath her nose the most amusing. I thought perhaps she hadn't realised that the pandemic was over.

"David. You are David, aren't you?" Not impressed, she has also read my CV and seen the photo of me that was attached to it. I nodded but kept tight-lipped. She's the clever one with psychic powers. I'll let her tell me everything.

"Oh David, you have been hurt, haven't you?" She sounded sad and concerned for my wellbeing. I didn't flinch, not even so much as an eye blink. "M, M, M. I keep seeing that letter, but the name I want doesn't begin with an M." Now she was getting spooky and sitting there with her eyes closed, slowly moving her hands as if she were caressing someone's body that was invisibly lying on the table in front of her. She suddenly opened her eyes. "Amanda. The woman who has hurt you is called

Amanda." Now she had my full attention. The promises I made to myself just a few seconds ago, not to divulge anything about my personal life, were taking flight and

disappearing before my eyes.

"Yes, her name is Amanda, and she certainly hurt me. What else can you tell me? Is there anything you can do to help mend this broken heart of mine?"

"Your heart isn't broken, David. It may be a little bruised and painful at the moment, but trust me. It is still in one piece. We all get hurt in life and deal with the problem differently. Some of us move on. Others become bitter and dwell on what they think of as rejection. They are lost, souls. They are like you, David. They need redirecting, that's all." Her words were warm and soothing to my ears, and deep down, I knew she was right. Sometimes it feels better to wallow in your self-pity and not accept the truth.

"I will read my tarot cards. They never lie. I will tell you what your love life holds." I watched as she shuffled a pack of colourful-looking cards. Then she spread them around the circular table and asked me to choose three but not to look.

I was still feeling very sceptical, so I simply moved the three cards that were closest to me and pushed them across the table to her. She stared at them as if she could see what lay beneath. I waited and then watched as she placed them in a specific order. "These three cards are everything. They will reveal all." She looked up at me and nodded, checking that I understood.

My heart was pounding as her hand hovered over the first card. She slowly and purposefully flipped it over. "The lovers." It seemed that she couldn't contain her smile. "You have met someone, and your desires are aligned. You will move closer together." I was already shaking my head. She couldn't be further from the truth. Madame Lydia saw my face and held her hand up. "You need to be patient. You must wait until all three cards have been turned and read."

Without waiting, she quickly moved to the next card and flipped it over. "The Empress. She is gentle and caring. She will help you nurture your feelings. Will bring you a deeper understanding of love and your true feelings." I clenched my teeth together. It was the only way I could suppress the laughter inside me. She was way off base, a million miles from the truth.

"This is your last card, David." Thank goodness, I thought. I needed to get out of this room. "This is the one that will connect all three." I assume that I read the card before she did. Because she stared down at it without saying a word for several seconds. "The Ten of Cups." She suddenly announced rather loudly. Yes, I know. I thought. I can read. "This is the perfect card. You are about to enter a time of true happiness."

That was me done. This woman was on a different planet from me. What's more, the sweet-scented josh sticks placed around the room had now finally given me a headache. "Thank you, Madame Lydia," I said, standing up and heading for the door. "I think I've heard enough for tonight."

"Please wait, David. We all need a little guidance from time to time." My hand was on the door handle, but I wasn't moving. Something was holding me in the room. Her voice was different. It was softer, and she sounded more sincere.

"Please just turn around for a moment, David." She wasn't asking. She was pleading with me. I obeyed her wishes. Something deep down was in control of me. I turned to face her. She was now standing just a few feet away from me. The scarf from her head and mask were gone. I could see those deep blue eyes once again. She was smiling warmly at me, and I was utterly captivated.

"Dorothy!" I gasped. "Was that really you beneath that veil of secrecy?" She smiled and nodded. "Yes, that was me doing what I do best. Masquerading as someone else. Sorting out their problems and ignoring my own." Her voice changed as if her throat suddenly tightened and was now choking her. I stretched forward and took her hand in mine. Her fingers were warm and trembling slightly. I gave them a gentle, reassuring squeeze.

"Would you kiss me, please, David?" I couldn't believe what I was hearing, but I didn't need to be asked twice. I leaned forward and met her waiting lips. Her arms went around my neck and mine around her slim waist.

The kiss was warm and passionate. Like nothing I have ever experienced in my life. "All of this was meant to happen. Believe me, tonight. We have just mended two broken hearts." She whispered in my ear as we held each other tightly.

THE CAPTURE

Inspired by: WHAT'S GOING ON.
Performed by MARVIN GAYE

"Mamma, why do we have to sit here? This ground is hard on my bottom, and I'm very thirsty." Her mother looked across at her seven-year-old daughter and tried to give her a reassuring smile. She didn't want to tell her the truth, that they were sitting there huddled together because the burly Russian soldier had ordered them to. "We are in the shade, Nadiya, and will eat and drink shortly." She smiled and pushed the hair out of her daughter's eyes.

She watched as her eldest child looked around at the other families being brought outside and ordered to sit in little groups.

"Are we going to die, Mamma?" The question took her mother totally by surprise. She was momentary dumbstruck, and her pulse rate quickened hearing her daughter's sad voice.

"We are not going to die, Nadiya." Her father answered her difficult question.

"So why do they have guns, and why do they wave and point them at us?"

"They are angry with us, that's all." Dmitry, her father, spoke quietly, hoping his voice would sound calm enough to satisfy his daughter's constant questions.

"Well, I don't like them," Nadiya replied abruptly.

"I don't like them either." Symon, her five-year-old brother who had been sitting listening, pipped up.

Just a few minutes ago, the four members of the Dudik family had been enjoying a simple Ukrainian Sunday lunch of boiled dumplings and cabbage when the Russian soldiers burst into their small second-floor apartment and changed all that. The startled family had knocked chairs over in their attempts to stand up quickly as ordered.

Symon and Nadiya instinctively ran to their mother for protection, clinging to either side of her long summery dress. She instantly wrapped an arm around each child. "You are safe with me." She had reassured them both, even though her heart was pounding in her chest. Then they had been ushered downstairs and outside into the warm sunshine, where they were now situated.

Gunfire within the apartment block made Nadiya jump and grip her mother's hand even tighter. Symon screamed, and his father knelt and hugged him. "It's okay." He whispered, knowing that the Russians had probably just shot their elderly neighbour Olek. He was the only person not outside yet.

"What has happened?" Dmitry yelled, still clinging to his son. An officer stepped forward. "It would seem that the man who lived next to you refused to leave his home."

"He was eighty-two. He was of no harm to anyone." Dmitry replied, looking up at the officer. "Perhaps you should tell that to the young soldier who he attacked with a kitchen knife?" Stubborn to the end, Dmitry thought to himself, shielding his son's face.

The Russian officer glared at Dmitry and

indicated that he should stand. He didn't hesitate. The last thing he wanted was to annoy any of them. "Are there soldiers down in the village? Perhaps waiting for us?" He smirked before turning towards the road that led down the hillside, the only way in and out of the small village for the residents living in the small apartment block. Dmitry shrugged. "I have no idea. We have not been down there for several days."

"You lie, my friend. Your wife walked down there with your pretty little daughter just yesterday. She bought bread and other items that she carried home in a basket." Dmitry didn't stop to consider his following words with care. He was annoyed the officer was toying with him.

"If you know this, you surely know what is happening in the village?" It was now the officer's turn to be angry he glared at Dmitry and pointed a grubby finger at him. "Your mouth could get you into trouble, my friend. I suggest you think more carefully before opening it next time." Dmitry didn't flinch. He stood his ground and said a silent prayer. He had seen the officer touch the handle of his pistol stuffed in his belt.

"I asked you the question because we believe there is a small unit of men in the area. Had you given me a straight answer, you might have saved some lives. Now, it seems l will have to call up the artillery, who will flatten your village to the ground to find out the truth." The officer stopped and thought for a second or two. "If they are there, perhaps they will run like rats deserting a sinking ship."

"Why?" Dmitry asked, sounding exasperated. "We are just simple people. We have nothing of value here. A little stored wheat, even our vegetables are rotting in the fields because the farmers are too afraid to go out and harvest them."

"That is war, my friend. It can be a nasty business. Certainly, when you are on the losing end." The officer gripped the handle of his pistol. His intentions were clear and menacing. Dmitry, worried for his family's safety, placed his hands in the air, showing the officer his palms. "Okay. Okay. There were soldiers down there a few days ago. But my wife didn't see any of them yesterday. They must have moved out. And that is the truth." The Russian stood shaking his head.

"Perhaps I should ask your little girl? What is her name?" The officer smirked. Dmitry moved his hands together as if in prayer.

"No, please! She wouldn't have seen anything. She is just a child."

"We all know that children see what adults sometimes do not. They have inquisitive eyes. She would have missed nothing on the trip down to your village. Now, what is her name?" The officer sounded impatient. Dmitry thought he might snap at any moment.

"Nadiya. My daughter's name is Nadiya. She is only seven years old." Dmitry was pleading. He was about to drop to his knees when he saw his wife walk towards them, holding Nadiya's hand. "I am Katya, and this is my daughter Nadiya. We, as you know, went down to the village yesterday morning. We saw no sign of Ukrainian soldiers, and no one I spoke with mentioned them. If they were there, then I believe that they have fled." The Russian officer nodded and pulled a satisfied face.

"Thank you, Katya. Being sensible, you have

just saved the lives of many people. Our intelligence reports are that a Ukrainian unit of fifty-plus men moved out at dawn yesterday. At least three hours before you and your young daughter ventured down the hill into the village."

Dmitry threw his hands up in the air. "So, why were you asking if you knew the answer?" The Russian officer laughed so loud that some of his men turned and looked towards the isolated Ukrainian family grouped beneath the pine trees.

"I enjoy playing games, my friend. This war is terrible enough as it is. So, I try to enjoy the lighter moments. I trust you don't have a problem with that?" Dmitry couldn't believe what he was hearing. This was a lighter moment? It made him feel sick that someone could play with him and his family like that.

"All of my experienced men are tracking them as we speak. That's why there is just one other officer in charge of these twenty young raw recruits with me. So few but enough to overrun your small village, I'm sure. Now the question is, what do we do with you and the rest of your neighbours?" The officer looked at Dmitry and then across to Katya. He gave a little shrug of his shoulders as if he couldn't quite decide.

Before she could react, Nadiya broke free of her mother's hand. "We could give you the bread that we have left over, and we have a few vegetables. Then you could go." She said firmly, looking up at the officer. He smiled before kneeling in front of her. Dmitry went to step forward. Katya caught his arm and held him back.

"I don't think you have enough bread to feed me and my men, young Nadiya." He rubbed the top of her head as he spoke. Nadiya didn't flinch. Instead, she held her tiny hand out. "Give me some money then, and I will go and fetch you some. Mamma will let me." She turned to face her mother. "You will, won't you, mamma?" Before her mother could answer. The officer had picked her up and swung her around in his arms. "We have food, thank you, but you are a kind girl to offer." Nadiya's father thought he saw a smile pass the officer's lips.

"I have a daughter back home in Western Siberia." He said to her, holding Nadiya high in the air. "Polina is older than you by two years, but she has the same beautiful blue eyes as you." He kissed the top of her forehead and placed her gently on the ground. Dmitry shuddered with distaste, hating the officer for touching his daughter, although he had been gentle with her.

As he straightened up, a single shot rang out. The Russian officer staggered forward as blood oozed from the nape of his neck. He turned, one hand automatically trying to stem the flow, the other pointing up at the flat roof of the apartment block. Another shot, this time hitting him in the chest. The force was enough to spin him around. He saw Nadiya, and her mouth was wide open. He knew she was screaming, but his senses weren't picking up the sound. He pushed Nadiya to the ground and fell on top of her.

As he lay there, two more bullets hit the officer. He had been forming a bridge with his body, keeping knees and elbows bent, but now his lifeless body slowly eased down on top of her. Her mother went to rescue her daughter from beneath the motionless body. Dmitry instinctively pulled her back. Another bullet pinged into the ground between Katya and the officer. She looked up and began shouting in the direction of their apartment. If it hadn't been for the quick thinking of her husband. She would be lying next to the dead Russian officer.

The young, inept Russian soldiers were in disarray. The remaining officer was shouting orders, but no one was listening to him. They ran for cover in all directions, some stopping to fire at a ghost. Someone that they knew was there, but someone that they couldn't see. The action would cost them their lives.

Those that managed to find some cover were now haphazardly firing at will. Bullets were smashing windows below the flat rooftop. The whitewashed wall at the front of the building was now peppered with pockmarks as the endless barrage of Russian gunfire continued, but the sniper kept finding his mark.

The other remaining officer went down, yelling and screaming for someone to come and drag him to safety. No one volunteered to help him. Clutching his stomach, he tried to get to his feet, but another loud pop from the rifle cracked open his skull.

Nine Russian soldiers and two officers were lying dead in less than ninety seconds, and three more were mortally wounded. The other unscathed soldiers now panicked and ran for the better cover of the pine trees. They were easy pickings for the sniper. Two more fell dead, crossing a section of open ground. Only a few were lucky enough to return to the forest where they had been hiding for the last two days. The area suddenly became eerily quiet.

In that short, violent time, Dmitry and Katya

had automatically shielded their son Symon with their bodies. Now it was time to rescue Nadiya from beneath the corpse of the Russian officer. Dmitry had mixed feelings about him. At first, the man had come across as uncaring and ruthless but had then shown compassion for their little girl. He had saved her life by throwing her to the ground and placing himself on top of her.

Dmitry felt his wife brush past him, one hand gripping her cotton dress, the other holding their son's little hand. "No, do not take Symon there. He is too young." Katya ignored his plea. She needed to help her daughter. He also wanted to be there, but he was still anxious about the shooter on the roof. He constantly looked up, praying under his breath that it was all over.

All three stood in front of the dead officer. Dmitry felt proud of his five-year-old son. He wasn't crying, he was just standing looking down. Symon didn't even seem scared as he shuffled his feet close to the body. But he still wanted him further away if they were going to pull Nadiya out.

He asked Katya to step back with Symon. She obeyed, and he knelt and started lifting the Russian officer. It was then that he heard his wife gasp loudly. He glanced up and saw her hand covering her mouth as she stifled a scream.

He followed her gaze towards their apartment block and saw the soldier slowly walking straight towards them. His rifle held low in a non-threatening manner. He even seemed to have a little cocky swagger about him. The frightening thing for Katya and Dmitry was this soldier wasn't Ukrainian. He was wearing a Russian uniform and getting closer by the second. Dmitry assumed the sniper had been left behind by the Ukrainian unit that had been in his village in an attempt to halt the Russian advance.

As Dmitry lifted the dead officer from his daughter, his hand touched something cold and metallic. Nadiya was lying there, her big blue eyes wide with fright. He put his finger to his lips and indicated that she stayed still and silent. He also stopped his wife from moving any closer. He saw tears in her eyes. She wanted to hug her daughter, but he knew any sudden movement might tip the soldier over the edge again.

The young Russian soldier was nearly upon them, yet still, he showed no sign of aggression. His rifle was still being carried at waist height.

"Why you are asking yourselves. So, I will tell you, my brother and I were forced here. We are not fighters, and he is now dead. Blown up stepping on a Russian landmine." He yelled, stopping several metres short of them. "My superiors give me no credit for my marksmanship. They think we are all green behind the ears. That we know nothing, now, they know nothing, and I know everything." He laughed loudly as he slowly lifted his rifle to his shoulder and took aim. He thought for a moment and lowered his rifle. "You bear witness to what has just happened. I cannot allow that. Life is unfair sometimes."

"No, please. Just go. Leave us in peace. We will say nothing. I promise." Dmitry pleaded with the young soldier, who was already shaking his head and raising his weapon.

The three shots that Dmitry fired all found their mark, and the Russian soldier slumped to the ground, dead. Katya screamed and flung her arms around their young son. Dmitry picked their daughter up and carried her over to her mother. The three hugged each other and cried together. Every emotion escaped from their weary bodies at the same time.

Dmitry stood staring at the lifeless young corpse in front of him. The pressure of war had made him snap, and his actions were that of a madman who was volatile and angry and now dead. As the immense tension of the past few minutes slowly ebbed away, tears ran freely down his face. When he had first put his hand on the officer's gun, he had prayed that he wouldn't need to use it.

"Life is unfair." He spoke to the dead soldier. "We didn't invite you into our country. Yet you came, killing, plundering, making demands on us, and taking what wasn't yours. Yes, life is unfair! But also, so is death."

NINETEEN THIRTY-FOUR

Inspired by: SOMEWHERE OVER THE
RAINBOW
Performed by JUDY GARLAND

I've lived in Russell County all my life, but these last three years have been hell. I can see nothing through the front windows. It's almost midday, but I am standing in almost darkness. The white picket fence that I know stands less than ten feet from here is completely invisible. The dust storm is unrelenting and has engulfed our tiny house again.

It seems that the fine dust has a way of penetrating through the wooden exterior of our home. It gets everywhere, in your eyes, down the back of your throat. Even breathing in through your nose is uncomfortable. The dust particles are slowly killing us all.

Our closest neighbours pulled out last year. Like us, they lost their crops of corn and wheat for the second year running and were on the brink of starvation. There was nothing that we could do for them. Our lives were no better. They bundled everything into their old ford and just up and left. We had no idea where they were going or if they even made it out of Kansas.

Martha and the kids are sat huddled together

in the far corner of the room with an old blanket over their heads. It gives them a little protection from the tiny gritty soil that scratches at your eyes and lodges beneath your eyelids, waiting for you to blink before bringing even more pain.

I can't remember the last time we went a whole week free of the dust. Just when we would think it had gone, it returned more powerful and ruthless. It's nearly the end of September, and I should be out there checking my corn. It's due for harvesting, but I don't know if it is even still standing. It certainly wasn't this time last year. By then, it had been completely flattened, and most of it had gone to waste.

I guess deep down, I know the true answer. My wife was right, and we should have pulled out as well. Any life must be better than this. Staying here and filling our lungs with the red dust, choking ourselves slowly to death.

Ronald, our son, has a high fever and trouble breathing. At just six years of age, he is a lifeless rag doll. He should be running around outside, climbing trees, and being yelled at by Martha or me. Instead, he is cradled in my wife's arms as she tries to comfort him. I can hear her quietly singing to him. It's enough to make me cry, but this wretched dust doesn't allow me even to do that. My eyes are so dry and caked. There is no moisture there, even for a single tear.

"Carl, Ronnie needs a doctor." Martha's words break into my thoughts and bring me back to reality. I want to turn around and scream at her. Tell her what a stupid remark that is. Instead, I shrug my weary shoulders before pointing through the window. She frowns back, and I know that she understands.

Going outside would be suicidal. We have heard of townsfolk being found lying dead on the pavement or even in their gardens because they went outside

My wife has found this life so hard to cope with. She was from a small town north of the County. She knew nothing about being a homesteader's wife. She was used to having running water in the house, not having to fetch it from a well outside. She was used to wearing smart clothes and a little make-up. I remember she had several hats for different occasions.

Now, she doesn't even own a lipstick or powder compact. She has also worn the same cotton dress for the past four years, which looks at least two sizes too big. It just hangs limply from her tired body. Sundays were different. On the Sabbath, she used to allow herself a change of clothing. Pretty dress and smart hat for church. That has all gone now. The dress is still hanging on the back of the bedroom door. She refuses to wear it, hoping that one day soon, everything will be normal again.

Martha is the dreamer among us. Before this wretched dust took over our lives, she would sit most evenings after supper on the front porch. Rocking slowly back and forth, gazing up into the night sky and yelling with excitement, when out of nowhere, a shooting star arrowed its way above the horizon. Now all I see is a crestfallen woman who has succumbed to this harsh life. It breaks my heart. I have given her nothing that I promised her. Even our love is slowly vanishing.

The morning sky is visible at last. I was up and about before anyone else was awake. Last night

Martha put Ronald to bed, leaving Nancy and me sitting listening to the constant rattling of the house as the dust bombarded the roof and walls. Nancy, at eight, is two years older than Ronald, and although I'm sure she doesn't understand what is happening to our lives, she is aware of how much damage this dust is doing to us.

As I step outside for the first time in two days, the sun is little more than a white oval disc, and there is hardly a patch of blue sky to be seen. I needed to keep busy, so I decided to check the crops. Even though I expected the worst, I hoped something might still be salvageable. However, I wasn't going to hold my breath. Especially when I saw the state of the barn. The large double front doors had collapsed, and the storm had deposited the reddish-brown soil so high inside the opening it was almost to the top of the door frame.

"Papa, can I come with you?" I turned to see Nancy standing in the doorway.

"Sure thing, honey. I'm going to check on the corn." I saw her pull a worried face. Even at her tender age, she had reservations. Nancy ran and caught me up. I offered her my hand and felt her tiny fingers wrap around mine.

"Will the horrible dust come back, Papa?" She asked as we walked away from the house, looking at the damage it had caused.

"I'm afraid it will, honey. We need some rain. Lots of it, in fact. And I can't see that happening any time soon." Her dark brown eyes looked sad as she considered my words.

"Will Ronnie get better soon?" Her question caught me off guard, even though I had only been thinking the same thing earlier this morning. I nodded and managed a half smile. "We hope so, Nancy. I might even be able to get him over to the docs later today. Once I've checked the crops."

"Mama would like that. She's worried sick about him."

"Me too, honey. Me too." I muttered under my breath, gripping her hand a little tighter.

We hadn't reached the field where the corn was planted yet. But I could see from here that there wasn't very much standing. There were scattered areas, perhaps, ten or twenty stalks standing defiantly in groups, as if some giant of a man had trodden them down but missed some of the more stubborn corn.

"Oh, papa!" Nancy gasped when we were close enough to see the true devastation. "It's okay, honey." I lied, wrapping my arm around her shoulder. "It's okay," I repeated as if saying it aloud would improve the situation. Nancy turned on her heels. I thought for one moment that she was going to run back to the house in tears, but she had heard her mother calling before I had.

"Carl. Carl." Martha was frantically waving her white apron to attract my attention. "Honey, go and check the field down by the creek." I stupidly pointed the way. She knew more about the creek than I did. Before this terrible drought and dust hit us, she and Ronnie were always down there. "I'll run back and see what your mother wants." My distraction hadn't worked. Nancy hesitated and was about to protest.

"Please, honey. I need to know the score. Check the crops and come back home." I watched her walk away. She stopped and looked back at me. I waved her on, gave her a thumbs up, and smiled. She was reluctant to go, but if Martha wanted me that urgently back at the house, something serious was up. Not having Nancy there seemed like a good precaution.

I ran as fast as I could. I hadn't even reached the barn when I saw Martha running towards me. "It's Ronnie. He's real sick this morning. He can hardly breathe." Tears were running down her cheeks, and she was shaking uncontrollably. I opened my arms to her, and she stepped into them. We hugged, and I kissed her forehead.

"Go back inside and sit with him. I'll get the pickup and drive him to Salina City. He'll be fine, Martha. I promise." She gave me a look that pained my heart. She knew better than I did that we might be just about to lose our only son.

The drive to Salina took me over two hours. The roads were covered in silt-like dust, and the journey was perilous. Twice I nearly slid off the road and ended up in the ditch. I had left Martha standing, watching us leave the farm. She needed to wait for Nancy to return. Then she would have the difficult task of explaining where we had gone.

I tried not to think of my wife and daughter's tears, especially if Martha told Nancy the truth, and I suspected she would. We had brought them both up that way. To be honest with each other at all times was one of the few rules we had in our household. Honesty, respectfulness, and politeness. Our lives were as simple as that.

I waited all day at St John's hospital for news of our son. Wondering all the time how he was doing, would he survive. As well as trying not to worry about the cost. How can people come up and ask whether I have a Blue Cross Plan policy? I had never heard of it, but from what I can gather, my son's illness could cost me a lot of money. I will sell the pickup and the tractor if need be.

By late afternoon a nurse advised me to go home and return tomorrow. In the meantime, they would do everything they could for Ronald. Reluctantly I left, knowing that at least he was still alive and holding on. I was at least taking something positive back home to my waiting family.

It was almost dark before I saw the faint glow of lights from the farm. I was hungry and completely drained. Every bone in my body ached, and what I wanted most in life was to hug Martha and Nancy and tell them what little I knew, hoping it would comfort them both.

They heard the car, and both rushed outside to greet me. I guess they were expecting to see both of us. Martha pulled Nancy close when she realised that I was alone. With her other hand clamped across her mouth, her eyes were wide and already filling with tears.

"He's okay. Ronnie's okay. He's in good hands. We can all go and visit tomorrow." I said, opening the little white gate and standing on the gravel path. Nancy broke free of her mother and rushed into my arms. Martha walked and joined us slowly. The look of worry on her face was still there. I nodded that it really was okay. She forced a smile and blinked away her tears.

During supper, I had been asked so many questions for which I had no real answers. I only knew that Ronald was alive and that the doctors and nurses were doing their best to keep him that way. I had insisted on an early night. We had a long day ahead of us tomorrow, and it wasn't going to be easy for anyone.

Sleep was evading me. I lay for hours staring at the ceiling, wondering where all of my dreams had gone. All of my promises to Martha and the children had been stolen from me. Why was life treating us so hard? We weren't bad people. We weren't asking for very much. Yet, we seemed to have less now than when we started.

For once, I wasn't the first one awake. I looked in Nancy's room, and her bed was empty. As always, she had made it and put her nightdress on top of the pillow. I assumed she was eager to go to the hospital to see her younger brother.

Martha followed me down the stairs and went straight into the kitchen to prepare breakfast. We both realised at once that Nancy wasn't in the house. I stepped outside. Perhaps she was on the porch having a few quiet minutes to herself.

"She's not there," I said to Martha standing in the open doorway.

"Have you checked the barn?" I shook my head. I knew there was no point in looking in there. I doubted that even a mischievous eight-year-old would be able to clamber over the great mound of soil blocking the entrance.

"There she is." I turned to see Martha pointing in the direction of the flattened crops. I stood watching as she ran towards us. I was feeling cross and angry. She had left the house without telling us. Anything could have happened to her. It was at that point I realised something wasn't right. She looked black from head to toe. Martha had already spotted the problem and was heading towards our daughter before I had even moved.

I caught Martha up and took her hand. We ran together, both wondering what the hell had happened to our daughter. As we got closer, Nancy stopped running and waited for us to arrive. She was now crying and holding her hands out.

"Papa, please don't be angry. I went back to the creek to see if it was still there. I took one of mama's baking tins. I wanted to collect what I had found. But I slipped." I looked across at Martha, and I could see that she was furious. We had enough on our plate with Ronald at the moment, without our daughter causing us problems like this.

I stepped in front of my wife and smiled at her. She frowned back at me. I could see that she was slightly bewildered. My smile wasn't a. *I'll handle this* smile. It was one of overwhelming joy. I took Martha's hand and squeezed it tightly. Then I turned back to Nancy. Her hands were now hanging limply at her side, and tears were still trickling down her blackened face, causing little rivulets to form on her cheeks. She was waiting for the scolding that she was expecting. I pulled Martha with me as I stepped towards our daughter.

"I'm not angry, honey. I love the way you look." I took her hand and gestured to Martha to take the other. We formed a tiny circle, and I knew both the women in my life were as perplexed as can be. Nancy looked up at her mother, who shrugged and waited. I didn't keep her waiting very long.

"I'm not cross, honey. You look like this….."
I began laughing. I couldn't control my emotions any
longer. "You look like this because that there dripping
from your dress and off your pretty little face, is
petroleum. It's oil, Nancy." I yelled at the top of my
voice and began jumping up and down. "You have
found oil on our land. Our lives are just about to
change forever." I had said enough, and my words
had sunk in. They both joined me, jumping, laughing,
and screaming. What a sight we must have looked.

Ronald pulled through and is home now and
growing stronger by the day. His sister is waiting on
him, hand and foot, always at his beck and call. It's
lovely to see. He was in the hospital for three weeks.
At one stage, it was touch and go, but like the rest of
the Arlen family, he is a fighter. He has proven that to
us all.

During that time, so much has happened.
Official-looking people have come and gone.
Professional oil riggers have surveyed different
sections of our land, and I'm told the initial signs are
excellent. Four more areas have been discovered, with
the prospect of more to come. Life for us all is slowly
getting better. Even the dust storms seem to be less
frequent all of a sudden.

When everything is finally sorted, and we can
move from this god-forsaken place, I have promised
Martha where ever we move to, the new house will
still have a front porch, and I know for sure her old
rocker will live on it.

She will be so happy to be outside once more,
breathing in the fresh air and not having to be cooped
up indoors. Heaven knows how long it will last, but at

the moment, life is wonderful. As my mother always used to say. *Every cloud has a silver lining.* I never really understood that as a child, but I will make it my job to explain it to my kids as best I can.

THE LEDGE

Inspired by: BRIDGE OVER TROUBLED WATER
Performed by SIMON and GARFUNKEL

The small two-seater plane flew low over the tops of the vast mountains. For those perched precariously on the narrow ledge, it seemed at first like their saviour had arrived. Help was on its way, they thought, and someone was coming to rescue them. Then, as it moved further away, it looked more like a giant bird gliding on the thermals, and that was the point they knew that they were alone.

Early that year, eleven people died, not far from their current position. In the unexpected warm weather, a glacier had collapsed and caused a massive avalanche. Theo knew from experience that this time they had been lucky. After hearing a distant rumble, he had led his two fellow climbers to safety. He had known an avalanche was imminent.

Not so long ago, the ledge they were on had been part of a snowy narrow mountain trail, with a high rock face on their right and a scary drop on their left. The avalanche hadn't been that big, but it had been enough to take away the path on either side. Marooning them and cutting them off in both directions.

The fast-moving snow had smashed down on the path and completely demolished it. The three were only there because the vast overhanging rock formation, that Theo had spotted, had sheltered them, allowing the thick blanket of snow to cascade either side, missing them all by just a few metres.

They were alive but stranded without any protection from the elements, and the temperature was dropping already. Unless Theo did something about the situation, the ledge would be their ice tomb. Liam was already grimly predicting their fate as he sat next to Kimberley, his wife, who was checking her ankle that she had twisted in her rush to get beneath the safety of the overhang.

Theo was busy looking through his rucksack. It was one of the two they now had. Liam hadn't been quick enough to pick his up. He had taken it off when they stopped briefly, complaining that something was digging into his back. Now it was gone. The avalanche had swept it over the edge.

Kimberley sidled up next to Theo and sat down. "It's impossible, isn't it?" Theo looked up from the light sticks he had been putting back into his rucksack. "Don't be such a defeatist, Kimberley. There is always hope while we are still breathing. We need to stay strong for each other." He looked away quickly. He didn't want her to see his eyes. She would have seen that he was lying through his snow goggles.

Kimberley gave him a hard stare. She was an experienced climber. She had been in difficult situations before, but nothing as bad as this, but nevertheless she knew the gravity of the mess they were in. Getting off the mountain was going to be near impossible. They needed a miracle, and Theo didn't have one in his rucksack.

Theo checked the ledge while the other two huddled together for warmth. He had told them not to move. The last thing he needed right now was to lose someone. He needed to keep them together and to keep morale at its highest. In this kind of situation, a negative person could cost lives. One stupid remark could change everything.

He edged his way slowly to the left. This was the way they had been coming before the avalanche hit. The loose snow beneath his boots crunched and sank into the deepest drifts. He looked across the yawning gap and guessed it was perhaps four metres, maybe even more. He shook his head disappointedly and moved carefully to the other side. He ignored both Kimberley and Liam as they looked up at him.

He could see at once without standing too near the edge that this looked better. It was probably less than three metres. The narrow path, their escape route, seemed frustratingly close but obviously not jumpable, especially with Kimberley's damaged ankle.

The three of them were not equipped for an overnight stay. They were already descending the mountain. This expedition had been planned as a challenging walk and an easy climb day before they went for the prominent peak two days from now.

Now they had no choice. It was out of their hands. This side of the mountain was east-facing. The natural light was behind the high peaks and fading fast. Theo knew he had perhaps an hour to explain his beliefs and keep them calm. Help wouldn't be coming until the morning. That was going to be hard to say, especially as he wasn't that convinced that help was coming at all.

"Listen up, guys. You don't need me to tell you how bad the situation is, but you are both experienced enough to know that if we work together, stay calm and focused, we will have a better chance of survival." Kimberley looked across to Liam, and their expressions said it all. "Listen to me. Everything will be different in the morning. We have a few provisions. Between us, we have plenty of energy snack bars and drinks. In the morning, we can review the cliff face better. It will be dark soon, and we need to try and keep warm enough through the night."

"I assume the rucksack we lost in the avalanche contained our main food supply?" Kimberley stared over at Liam. She knew the answer already. She also knew that he was carrying both their mobile phones. Something that they hadn't mentioned to Theo yet.

Kimberley and Liam had been married for five years this month, and this trip to the north-eastern section of the Alps was supposed to celebrate their anniversary. They had always wanted to climb an area within the famous Dolomites close to the Italian and Austrian border.

Theo smiled at Kimberley. She didn't mince her words. If she thought it, she said it. Simple and straight. He liked that about her. "Afraid so about the food. The other bad news is, my mobile got damaged when I caught my lower back on a jagged rock beneath the overhang." Theo couldn't miss the expressions on both of their faces.

"What! What is it you're not telling me?" Kimberley lifted her goggles onto her forehead. "Both of our mobiles were in Liam's rucksack." Theo couldn't believe his ears. "You are kidding me. What were you thinking? You know the score. We always keep electronic devices on our person. Not in our bloody rucksacks, for that exact reason. Bloody hell, guys, you are both supposed to be experienced climbers, not bloody day trippers." Theo stood and walked to the edge of the narrow ledge. He leaned over and peered down through the fading light into the seemingly bottomless chasm.

Liam and Kimberley both stood in unison, Kimberley wincing from her damaged ankle. They both had had the same terrible thought. Theo was aware that they were standing close behind him. "Stay put, guys. It's a little bit soft and crumbly here. It might not take all of our weight." He turned to face them. Seeing their facial expressions, he nodded an okay and walked back. Kimberley had been terrified. She hugged Theo and whispered *sorry* into the side of his neck.

"Right then. I've checked my bag." He stated positively. "Let's see what joys yours will reveal?" He stretched his hand out and waited as Kimberley fumbled to pick it up. Once he had unbuckled the straps, he began pulling items out.

"Two thermal blankets. That will be cosy." He chuckled, looking up for a reaction. They were smiling at him. The tension of a few minutes ago had gone. He pulled at a large piece of material and unravelled it. "We have a flag. With a big red heart on it." Theo frowned. It was an unusual item to bring on such a trip.

"It's our fifth wedding anniversary this week. The idea was, we were going to place it at the highest peak that we managed to climb." Liam explained, looking towards his wife.

"Nice. Very romantic." Theo hadn't meant to sound quite so sarcastic, but the flag was pretty big and taking up a lot of room in Kimberley's bag. "Good, more light sticks." He enthused, holding them aloft. "We have ten in total now."

"Kimberley's idea," Liam explained. "She does like to be prepared for everything. She probably has tinned fruit and a can opener there, too." He was now smiling. They were in a dangerous situation, but it suddenly felt like the couple was bonding with their guide.

Theo carried on emptying Kimberley's rucksack. There was no tinned fruit, but he found four bananas, some dried meat strips, and packets of assorted nuts. Liam was right. Kimberley certainly does come prepared. She would have been hauling too much stuff if this trip had gone to plan. Now, she was carrying enough supplies to help them through the night and part of tomorrow.

Theo was already awake when the first chink of morning light seeped between the uneven array of distant peaks directly in front of him. From where he sat, they looked like the bottom jaw of a giant dinosaur baring its jagged, snarling teeth back at him. He looked over to where Kimberley and Liam were huddled together. He couldn't tell who was who. They had given Theo one of the thermal blankets and shared the other one.

One of them threw the blanket off the second he moved, and they stood. "Morning, Theo," Kimberley said, showing no sign of a restless night but still hobbling on her twisted ankle.

"Morning. No better then?" He asked, pointing down to her foot. Kimberley shook her head.

"She won't tell you this," Liam began. "but she was in a lot of pain last night." Kimberley nudged her husband.

"Thanks, Liam. That's the sort of info I need to be told." He looked straight at Kimberley. "You must keep me in the picture at all times. If it's causing you a problem, I need to know. Understood?" She nodded and slowly sat back down.

"Right, we need to eat and drink. Kimberley, will you be mother and put us some sort of breakfast together?" Theo saw the pained expressions on their faces as they looked at each other. He turned away, cursing beneath his breath. He had, without realising it, hit a nerve. He carried on as though nothing had happened and passed Kimberley the rucksack containing the food.

Liam sat beside her with his fists clenched inside his thick thermal gloves. He knew what that one solitary word was doing to his wife inside. They had been trying for nearly three years to have a baby, but nothing was happening in that department. They had already decided to have tests carried out when they arrived home from this trip. Liam felt for her. She was always blaming herself. His telling her *it takes two to tango* always fell on deaf ears. She needed to stop beating herself up.

As Liam sat staring out into the vast white wilderness, he suddenly remembered the note. He allowed himself a wry smile. He leaned forward to speak to Kimberley but quickly pulled back. There was no point in mentioning what he had been planning. There was nothing to be gained. It was, after all, supposed to be a surprise for their wedding anniversary. A special romantic meal for two.

Before they left their rented chalet down in the valley and began their adventure of a lifetime, Liam had spoken with Pierre, a local chef who had come highly recommended. Between them, they had planned the surprise meal right down to the last detail. Liam even gave him a spare door key to the chalet, allowing him to prepare the food beforehand.

The note was supposed to give Pierre an idea of when they were hoping to arrive, and if he could, Liam would call him on their descent to help with the timing. That, of course, was not going to happen now. Nonetheless, Liam could hardly control his feelings because, in his note, he had mentioned to the chef which areas they were walking and which peak they were hoping to climb.

By now, help must be on its way. He went through the different scenarios in his head. Pierre would have waited, perhaps a couple of hours, and then he would have alerted the authorities. It would have been dark by then, so they couldn't do much until now. Liam was still torn. He wanted to say something. It would give them a little boost, but wouldn't it be great to shout surprise when the rescue party turned up?

They had finished eating the bananas and the energy bars that Kimberely had handed around when Theo suddenly stood up. "Listen up, guys. I'm going to climb up around the overhang. I've got an idea, but I need your flag?" They both nodded in unison and watched as he removed it along with some of the light sticks. He was going to free climb. It was dangerous, if not a little foolhardy, but something needed to be done.

After twenty minutes, Theo was out of sight of Kimberley and Liam He gauged that they were perhaps fifty metres below him. He had done well. He had managed the overhang easier than he thought and had climbed almost to the top of the jagged pinnacle.

It had taken its toll. He was utterly exhausted. His fingers ached, and his feet felt numb. Shivering with the cold, he spread the flag out and sat waiting in the most prominent position he could bear. The sharp cold wind cut like endless razor blades through his clothing. He would stay as long as he could.

Below him on the ledge, Kimberley was upset and tearful. His inappropriate mother comment to her earlier was still gnawing away at her. Liam understood and wrapped his arm around her. "You're not alone in all of this, Kim. Through all of your darkest times, I'm here for you every step of the way. I love you, and together we will make it." He held her even tighter as guilt about the romantic dinner washed over him.

Theo was at the point of giving up and going back down when he heard the faint sound of a distant engine. He listened carefully, trying not to become over-excited. He needed to be sure, and then suddenly, there it was, rising slowly over the top of the jagged dinosaur teeth and facing him.

He gently stood and broke two of the light sticks and waved them in the air. Even through all the swirling snow that the rotor blades were making, the pilot was close enough for Theo to see him give a thumbs up before pulling away and disappearing out of sight.

Down on the ledge, Kimberley and Liam hugged each other with excitement. They were safe, and a rescue party was on its way. They waited patiently for Theo to scramble back down. He took his time. A wrong footing now would be disastrous after everything he had just been through. Once back on the ledge, all three embraced and congratulated each other.

"I hope you don't mind, but I left your flag up there as a marker." They both smiled and shook their heads. Theo nodded and removed the remainder of the stick lights from his bag. "Two each, just in case they can't find our exact position. Now, we sit and wait." All three sat silently wrapped in their blankets. Theo's thoughts were of his fellow climbers. He was still thinking about his remarks that caused the friction. Perhaps he would ask Liam once they were down safely.

Several hours had ticked away. During that time, to help their circulation, Theo had made them stand and move about. He had them do silly exercises, touching their toes and swinging their arms around. Knowing that help was coming, they also ate the rest of the meat strips and numerous handfuls of nuts.

Liam stood up first. He could hear talking, but no one was visible at the moment. Theo and Kimberley joined him, looking left and right. They were confused. The voices seemed to be all around them. Then suddenly, rescuers wearing their traditional bright red helmets and matching insulated jackets appeared on either side of the ledge.

Theo indicated that Liam and Kimberley stood still before walking carefully towards one of the groups. He knew just how excited they were, but he didn't want any sudden stupid movement to cause a problem. "Are we glad to see you guys?" He smiled wearily across at them.

"Are you Liam?" One of the rescuers asked. Flabbergasted, Theo shook his head and hooked his thumb over his shoulder. "That's Liam back there, holding his wife's hand." The rescuer stepped to one side so that he could address Liam. "Pierre sends his compliments." The man in the red helmet beamed. Liam looked a little sheepish but waved back.

"I'll explain later. I promise." He quickly said to Kimberley before she could start her interrogation. He then wrapped his arms around her. "It's okay. We're safe now." He whispered into her neck.

The rescue party quickly determined which group had the shortest distance to traverse between them. Kimberley watched, fascinated, as a person in each group took out what she first thought was a mobile phone. When she saw the little red dot, she quickly realised that it was some kind of laser meter. "Three metres." One of them shouted. She watched as the climber on the other side knelt down and aimed his meter towards the ledge. "Five metres." He yelled across the divide, looking disappointed at the same time.

Two men at the back of the group stepped forward with a long aluminium ladder. They attached a rope at the far end before vertically pushing the other end of the ladder into the snow. Then between them, they slowly and carefully lowered the ladder across the void. As it nestled gently on the other side, the man who had spoken with Theo and Liam stood on the first rung and pushed down hard with his foot. Without another thought, he walked carefully across to the ledge.

Theo and Liam shook his hand while Kimberley threw her arms around his neck and kissed him. His face now matched his attire. "We need to move." He said, stepping back, trying not to meet her eyes.

"Kimberley has a twisted ankle," Theo informed the red-faced man. He now had to look at her. "How bad is it?"

"I'm not sure I can walk across there because of the gaps in the rungs." She replied, her voice breaking up as she realised her predicament. Her rescuer nonchalantly shrugged his shoulders. "Marco, bring a stretcher over. The lady cannot walk." A young lad carrying a canvas stretcher was on the ledge in no time. Kimberley hadn't even seen him make the journey. He was that quick.

"So, Miss Kimberley. We will simply strap you in and carry you over ourselves." He gave her a wry smile and placed the ladder at her feet. She looked down at it and then back up at the man saving her life.

"I believe you are already late for dinner. Pierre is my brother and the best chef within a hundred kilometres. I would suggest we don't keep him waiting any longer."

Kimberley looked across at her husband. He smiled back before shrugging and saying. "Happy anniversary darling."

SIT WITH ME AWHILE

Inspired by: CREEP
Performed by RADIOHEAD

It was the last Friday of August, and he had been visiting the same park bench since the beginning of June. He often arrived early to claim the seat he wanted for himself. Usually, when he arrived, he would put his feet up, stopping other people from sitting next to him. He ignored the looks when others stood before him, silently demanding that he put his feet down and sit up.

Only once in all his visits to the bench had someone challenged him and asked him to move over. Two words from his double-pierced lips and his scowling glare had sent the elderly woman on her way, muttering about the younger generation and what the world was coming to.

He didn't want anyone sitting next to him, well, he did, but it certainly wasn't an old woman with her canvas shopping trolley. He didn't need the distraction of someone eating their lunch or feeding the never-ending number of pigeons that flocked to the green oasis in the middle of the busy city. He just wanted one thing, and one thing only.

Yesterday, he had calculated that he had been

here at least fifty times and still hadn't spoken to her. He didn't even know her name yet. All the times she had sat on the bench opposite him reading her book, he hadn't dared approach her. He had wanted to so often, but he just couldn't bring himself to make that first move.

Thomas Spencer was anything but confident about himself. At twenty-one, he had done nothing with his life so far. To most people seeing him for the first time, they perceived his looks and dress sense as weird. He belonged nowhere. With his ripped jeans and black leather jacket festooned with chains and padlocks, plus his Doc Martens boots, he was definitely an outcast in society.

He never stopped to help himself. If he felt he needed a boost, his way of dealing with it was to get another tat or a piercing. This month his arm has been inked twice, and his nose has been introduced to a septum ring piercing. Thomas never had anything good to say about himself, but he was in love, and being in love can often change a man.

Thomas checked his phone, and it was twelve-fifty already. He was later than usual, thanks to a minor accident when the bus he was aboard decided to argue with another one coming in the other direction. By now, he would have been sitting waiting in the park. Now, having abandoned the chaos and mayhem the two buses caused, blocking the road and holding up the rest of the traffic. He was in a hurry, walking quickly, almost running to try and arrive before she did.

He jumped over the low wall that guarded the park from the interlopers of the busy high street before sprinting across the grass. Flower beds, dog walkers, and joggers were everywhere, all directly in his path. It appeared he was running an assault course, not going to see the woman of his dreams.

The path in front of him straightened, revealing an avenue of trees and benches on either side along the route. Thomas stopped and stared. She was there, she was early and, even worse, someone was with her. This had never happened before. He panicked and stepped to one side, using the trunk of a sprawling oak tree to hide behind.

He watched the couple as they sat talking and laughing. Suddenly, for the first time ever, he didn't want to be here anymore. All of his waking hours were about this moment. Seeing her, watching her graceful movements, taking in every aspect of her. Now, someone else was where he should be. Sharing her thoughts, sitting next to her, and being captivated by her lovely smile. He had dreamed of that moment so often, and now it had been stolen away from him.

Thomas was angry and frustrated, but he wasn't about to give in. He wouldn't let this man, this rival spoil his day. She was sitting there. That was the main thing. He needed to regain his composure and act naturally. He jiggled with his white earbuds and walked calmly to the bench opposite them. He would normally have music blasting through them, but not today. It was part of his deception plan. To sit and pretend to enjoy different tunes while watching her every movement.

As soon as he arrived at the park bench, the man he considered his rival stood to leave. "Right then, Melanie, I'm heading back to the office. I'll leave you to finish your book and see you later."

Thomas was beside himself. He knew her name, and it suited her. "Melanie. Melanie. Melanie." Her name tripped off his tongue as he smiled to himself with satisfaction.

He sat back on the wooden bench and pretended to close his eyes. All the time, leaving just enough of a gap to watch her. He nodded his head to the soundless music and drummed his fingers on his knees. His squinted eyes watched her as she read her book. He struggled to focus correctly as he desperately tried to read the title.

He opened his eyes fully. She was too engrossed in her reading to notice what he was doing. He leaned forward slightly to see better. At that moment, Melanie raised her book as she adjusted her position, allowing Thomas to see the cover better. "Pride and Prejudice!" He mumbled to himself. "Who reads that sort of old twaddle nowadays?" He felt a pang of disappointment. Discovering her name had now been surpassed by her choice of reading matter.

Yet, he still couldn't take his eyes off her. Knowing that she liked reading Jane Eyre only fuelled his feeling that she was better than him. She was still up there on the high pedestal he had placed her on the first day he saw her. She was unique in every way, her body movement and how she carried herself when walking.

Thomas closed his eyes and tried to conjure up a picture of her. In his head, he contemplated different scenarios, some so weird that it made him smile. "Are you listening to anything good?" A soft voice whispered near the side of his cheek. Startled, he opened his eyes and his mouth as well. No words escaped from his lips as he stared straight back at

Melanie. "May I?" She asked, pointing to the vacant spot next to him. Thomas nodded and watched as she lowered herself into the space.

As he took a deep breath to compose himself, the sweet vanilla fragrance from her long raven hair filled his head and took over his senses. Then their legs gently touched, and she made no attempt to break the connection, making his heart race and his head spin even more.

His brain seemed so dysfunctional that he couldn't think of anything to say. He just sat there staring and realising for the first time just how beautiful she really was. Her brown eyes were much darker than he thought, almost ebony that glistened like two shiny black pools as she looked straight at him. He was captivated, as well as speechless.

"An introduction would be a good start." She teased him, smiling and melting his heart.

"Thomas. I'm Thomas Spencer. Most people call me Tommie." He puffed his cheeks out, unable to conceal his nervousness. Melanie was still smiling as she raised her hand. "Melanie Palmer. My close friends call me Mel." Thomas took her waiting hand. It was soft and warm, and he felt his fingers tingle as they touched.

"It's a pleasure to speak with you at last." She added, still holding his hand and squeezing it ever so lightly. Thomas frowned. What did she mean at last? Melanie saw the look of confusion on his face. "I'm guessing, but I bet you've been here, sat on this bench about forty times." She waited for his reaction. In his head, he corrected her. "Fifty-one, actually." Thomas shrugged away her statement. "Well, I like sitting here, watching the world go by," he replied eventually. As she released his hand, she gave him a knowing look.

"Spying is nearer the truth."

"Spying?" He responded, letting a little grin edge its way across his lips.

"Yes, spying. You turn up almost every day. I sit over there," she pointed to the empty bench opposite, "and you sit here and watch me read my book, drink my water, eat my lunch."

"I don't know what you mean," he protested, his smile broadening. Melanie sat back and thought for a second. "Quick answer. What sort of water do I drink?"

"Sparkling," Thomas replied without hesitation. Melanie shrugged and raised her hands palms up. "I rest my case." She laughed.

The awkward silence that surrounded the bench didn't last very long. Melanie checked her phone and stood to leave. "I must go. I will be late back at the office." Thomas stood as well. Once again, he was tongue-tied. His head was sending him so many messages that he couldn't put his words in the proper order.

Melanie came to his rescue. "If you fancy going for a drink tonight, meet me here at eight sharp. My treat." She didn't wait for an answer, although she clearly heard him shout. "Right then. Eight it is." Just before she stepped through the park gate and back into the real world.

Thomas jumped onto the bench and stretched on tiptoe just in time to see her crossing the busy street and turning the corner. "Wow." He shouted at the top of his voice before leaping over the back of the bench. He walked briskly through the park, like a lottery winner on his way to collect his money. He couldn't contain himself.

Then, from out of nowhere, doubt began to creep into his head slowly. Had that really just happened? What did she see in him? She was so beautiful, so majestic. What was she doing asking him out on a date? He stopped and looked around. There wasn't another soul in the park. That just added to his misery. He felt alone, abandoned even.

By the time Thomas had finally made it home, the late afternoon sun was almost dropping behind the row of houses where he lived. It had taken him nearly two hours to get home. At first, he had wandered aimlessly around the park's perimeter, thinking things through, and trying to believe in himself. When he eventually left the quiet green sanctuary of the park, he still had problems with his self-esteem.

He should have been happy and ecstatic. What he had wanted most in this world had just happened. The woman who occupied his thoughts day and night had spoken with him, even invited him out for a drink. He now had some big decisions to make, and some weren't going to be easy for him. What was going around in his head scared him half to death.

"Eight o'clock sharp, she had said," Thomas recalled her words under his breath while looking down at his phone. "Seven forty-five, and there are the park gates. I'm nice and early. Great!" He felt better about himself. He had a fresh spring in his step, and even his mother commented on how different he looked. He also wanted to ensure he was there first, sitting on the bench, seeming calm and relaxed.

As he approached the straight path with the perfectly spaced trees that led to their rendezvous point, he saw a woman sitting on the bench that he now considered theirs, but it wasn't Melanie. He slowed his pace taking in every detail of the mysterious woman.

He made a decision and walked straight on by, not even glancing in her direction, and then something made him stop and turn. The woman was standing looking at him. He walked back, still trying to grasp the situation.

"I thought you were going to stand me up there for a minute." He immediately recognised Melanie's voice but was still very confused. She looked utterly different, dressed in shredded jeans and a dark t-shirt and wearing thick black mascara and black lipstick. Her hair was so different as well. It was now purple, short, and spiky.

"I'm sorry I didn't recognise you dressed like that." He was now standing right in front of her, looking her up and down.

"I could say the same about you. What's with the smart trousers, striped shirt, and casual jacket? And my god, where has the lovely nose septum and your two lip piercings gone? What have you done to yourself?" They both stood staring at each other, Melanie shrugging her shoulders in disbelief and Thomas scratching his head.

They sat down and leaned towards each other without saying a word. The silence was awkward, and neither knew where to start. Thomas cleared his throat to speak, but Melanie took the opportunity to start first.

"All the times I've seen you sat on that bench opposite. "She pointed across the park path. "I've been envious of you."

"Envious of me?" He butted in, looking puzzled. Melanie nodded.

"Yes, because you are what I've always wanted to be, a rebel, eccentric, a non-conformist. But most of all, you are a free spirit." Thomas began shaking his head and waving his hand at her.

"No, Melanie, I'm none of those things. I'm nothing compared to you. You are witty and clever, and you have a job that helps you to be independent. You read intelligent books." Thomas paused for thought. "It was Pride and Prejudice today. Another time I saw you reading Emma, also by Jane Austen. I had to Google her name to find out who she was.

Melanie began to laugh and then dug deep into the canvas shoulder bag that she had with her. She produced a book and held it up for Thomas to see. Then to his surprise, she peeled the cover away to reveal a different one. "As you can see, it's not actually Pride and Prejudice. It's called A Gothic Curse. It's about vampires in Rome in the sixteenth century. Jane Austen is a bit twee for me." Thomas stood silently, staring at the dark features of a bat with the title written in blood red. He was at a loss on how to respond.

"The manager at the Estate Agents where I work would freak out if he saw me reading this." She shook the book to make her point. "He doesn't even allow various coloured nail polish. It has to be red and nothing else."

"So, you're Miss Prim and Proper during the day and Dracula's Daughter at night?" He snickered softly at his silly remarks.

"That's about the size of it," Melanie replied gleefully. Seemingly pleased with his description of who she was. Thomas began to feel uncomfortable. For over two months, he had been obsessed with this woman, and she had shattered his dreams in a matter of minutes. He didn't want her to be like him. The whole reason he was attracted to her was her normality.

He was becoming cross, and his feelings were boiling up inside him. He had wasted all of this time visiting the park, too afraid to speak with her because she would see him as some kind of freak, and all the time, she was a screwball, a misfit herself. And too ashamed to show the world who she really was. This wasn't going to work. Going for a drink dressed like this was not what he wanted.

Melanie moved to put her book away, but Thomas stepped forward and took it from her. "May I?" He asked, gripping the spine. Melanie nodded and released her hold. Thomas flicked through the pages as if he was half expecting something to jump out at him. He took a closer look at the front and traced his finger around the outline of the bat. Then he turned it over and read the back.

"I have to go, Melanie." He said, still holding her book firmly. She frowned. She didn't understand what was going on.

"Have I done something wrong?" she asked, her forehead furrowed, and she looked confused. Thomas shook his head and stepped to one side.

"No, you've done nothing wrong, Melanie. In

fact, the trouble is me. I have never been happy with myself. Throughout life, I have blamed everyone else for my problems, my attitude, and this chip on my shoulder." He glanced across to his upper arm. "So, no, you've done nothing wrong. On the contrary, you have helped me without knowing it. In the last few minutes, I've come to realise that you can't tell a book by its cover." And with that, Thomas handed A Gothic Curse back to her. Before adding. "Enjoy the rest of the story."

THE OPEN DOOR

Inspired by: RESPECT
Performed by ARETHA FRANKLIN

The children were out from under her feet at last. Susan, her younger sister, had picked them up and taken them both to the cinema, she had no idea what they were going to see, but at least now the house was quiet once more. She had needed the break for her own sanity. Everything seemed to be getting on top of her at the moment.

Christina inhaled the silence as she turned around and around in the lounge of her house. It felt so good to be free for a few hours before Ben and Natasha returned. They were both such a handful. Ben was nearly eleven, Natasha was eight last month, and the school summer holidays had only just started, and Christina was already feeling the pressure.

She had just sat down with her cup of coffee when she heard the front door open. "They can't be back home already?" She moaned under her breath, as she waited for her two children to come crashing through the lounge door and steal her precious moment from her. Christina sat up when she realised that it wasn't the children. It was too quiet in the hallway. There was no excitement, no shouting, and squealing.

Christina stood as soon as she saw who her interloper was. "What are you doing home this early?" She asked, looking puzzled.

"Hi darling, have you had a good day at the office?" Steve, her husband, bitched, disregarding her question. Christina put her coffee down and walked over to him. She put her arms around his neck and kissed him on his cheek. "So, have you?" she teased.

"Actually, yes. I landed the Zimmerman contract. We've been after it for over a year now."

"Oh, darling, that's wonderful." Christina didn't know what the Zimmerman contract was all about, but her husband was ecstatic, so that was good enough for her. Steve pulled away from his wife when he realised how quiet the house was.

"Where are the kids?" He asked, looking perplexed. Christina gave him a mischievous smile. "Sue has taken them to see a film. We have the house to ourselves." She raised her eyebrows, and her smile broadened as she waited. Steve was already shaking his head.

"No, can do. I promised some of the lads from work I would meet them down the pub in half an hour. We thought we should celebrate finally being their accountants after all this time." Christina turned on her heels and stormed out of the room. Steve held his arms aloft. "What! What's the problem?" He yelled after her. In seconds his wife was back, her face red with anger, and her finger pointed straight at him. "I'll tell you what the problem is. You take me for granted too often, and I'm not appreciated around here. You just want a cook and a cleaner. Well, that isn't me. Not anymore."

Steve didn't bother to defend himself. This wasn't the first time Christina had gone off on one, and he suspected that it wouldn't be the last. She could stay home and wallow in her self-pity while he did what he wanted. He just needed to get out of the house. These confrontations weren't healthy, and they always ended in stalemate.

"If you go, Steve, I swear I won't be here when you return." She shouted angrily at his back as he opened the front door. He turned towards her and half smiled. "I'll see you later, Christina." She hunched her shoulders and closed her eyes at the door closing. She was seething at his arrogance, and he was almost laughing at her as he left.

Having called Susan and asked her to bring the kids back, Christina hurried up the stairs and pulled a suitcase from the bottom of her wardrobe. She then dashed around between bedrooms grabbing whatever she thought was necessary. Once the case was bulging and she had struggled to zip it closed, she sat on her bed and made a call.

While she waited for her younger sister to bring Ben and Natasha home from the cinema, she began making plans. Steve was in for a shock when he walked through the door later. There would be no one home and no note explaining where they were. She needed to make a point, and this was going to be explosive.

Susan arrived carrying Natasha, who was in floods of tears after being dragged away before the end of her current favourite film. Ben was the complete opposite. He wasn't fazed by being brought home early. He had never wanted to see Minions anyway. He would have preferred to watch the film about the crocodile taking a bath that he had seen on his iPad.

Christina didn't explain herself to her younger sister. Instead, she thanked her and showed her the front door. Susan didn't ask any questions. Growing up together, she had seen that look on Christina's face a hundred times. She knew better than to query what was going on.

"Okay, guys, listen up." Christina began once she had them both seated on the couch and Natasha had stopped crying. "We're going on a little trip."

"Where to Mommy? Disneyland?" Ben asked excitedly. His mother shook her head. "No, but somewhere really nice. It's not far from here."

"Do they have a cinema?" Natasha asked, still sniffing and wiping her nose with the back of her hand.

"I think they do, Natasha, yes."

"So, can we go and see the rest of the Minions?" Natasha was now smiling, her rosy cheeks glowing and flushed.

"We'll see, babe. We need to get there first." Christina looked away from Natasha as a little niggle of doubt crept into her head. It lasted no more than a couple of seconds because Ben was now asking where exactly they were going.

"Devon, we're going down to Devon for a short break. A little holiday."

"Is daddy coming?" Ben asked, smiling at the thought of going on holiday.

"Not this time, darling. He has a lot of work on at the moment." Christina stood and ushered them both upstairs.

"Why is daddy always working? He doesn't even take me to football anymore." Ben flopped down on his bed, the excitement of going on holiday quickly fading. Christina ignored his question and instead tried to motivate her young son.

"Come on, help me choose what other clothes you need. I've already packed some. Then we can go and help your sister." She released a huge sigh. She knew he was right and that Steve wasn't the father to his children that he used to be. He wasn't the same man that she had married.

The motorway was extremely busy, and it seemed as if the whole country wanted to visit Devon, and they were all in a rush to get there. Christina considered turning back to Bristol, but she knew from her satnav that she was well past halfway, so she kept going. Even though thoughts of doubt kept churning through her head, leaving her with a twinge of guilt, she drove on.

Christina left the motorway, joined the A30, and headed towards Okehampton, her final destination. The dual carriageway seemed just as busy with cars and heavy goods vehicles, but she was still making good progress and determined to get there in two hours and beat Steve's best time by ten minutes.

Natasha asking if they could stop for something to eat and drink changed all of that. Christina knew they both must be hungry and knew exactly where to go. The Hog & Hedge, they did wonderful Cheddar toasties for the kids, and she could have a hog and cheese toasty herself. More importantly, the junction turnoff was coming up.

Steve came through the front door of their house like a whirlwind. He hadn't even closed it before he was calling for his wife. "Chrissie, I'm back." He stood in the hall and listened. He knew she was angry with him, but it wasn't like her to sulk.

On the contrary, he had been expecting her to come and face him, give him another ear bashing. He checked his watch. It was twenty-past five, so the kids should also be home by now. Then it slowly dawned on him what it was he had missed, what he hadn't seen. He turned and opened the front door. He was right. Her car had gone.

He ran up the stairs and opened her wardrobe first. Her pink suitcase wasn't there anymore, and it was then that he saw the four coat hangers lying on the bed. His heart raced while his brain tried hard to make sense of the situation. Everything was a jumble. He was thinking of so many things at the same time. Sure, she threatened to leave, but he didn't believe her. She would never do something so dramatic as walkout and take the kids as well.

Steve tried calling his wife's mobile, but she had turned it off. He then called her sister, Susan, who confirmed that Christina had phoned her whilst in the cinema and ordered her to bring the children home at once. She knew she wasn't happy about something, but she didn't know what it was or what was going on. That was all she could tell him. Christina had not explained her actions. As Steve disconnected, he suddenly remembered the phone monitoring app that they had installed on Ben's phone without his knowledge. Christina had insisted that it was a good idea even though they had never used it.

"Devon! Bloody hell, she does want to get away from me." Steve mumbled to himself. "Devon, so it's Okehampton and The White Hart Hotel." Steve stood nodding, happy that he now knew where they were heading. At the end of the day, it was the most logical place for her to go. It was one of their favourite UK destinations. Nice and quick to get to, somewhere for them both to relax. They usually went there three or four times a year.

Steve was in his car and joining the M5 motorway within ten minutes. He drove within the speed limit and didn't want his feelings to cloud his judgement. Now he could track her via Ben's mobile, and he was more confident about exactly where she was going, he wasn't feeling quite so anxious. However, it didn't stop him from trying to figure out what was happening inside his wife's head. Where was all of this anger coming from?

As he turned into George Street, he started looking for somewhere to park. He saw a delivery van pulling out from behind the back of The White Hart Hotel, and although he knew he shouldn't do it, without hesitation he parked there. He was only planning on being a minute. As if to prove the point, he ran back down the road to the front of the building.

Looking around, he couldn't see Christina or the children. Perhaps they were in their room or had gone to stretch their legs. He knew there was a park close by. Natasha, in particular, loved going there as they had an adventure playground down in the far corner.

"May I help you, sir?" Steve turned to face a

young waitress, smiling pleasantly at him. He returned the smile and regained his composure, still breathing heavily from his run.

"I'm looking for my wife and children. I think they arrived here today." He placed his hand on his chest for a little comfort.

"I don't think so, sir. We are fully booked, we have a wedding party in, and they have almost taken over the place." Her smile altered slightly as she showed a bit of sympathy to the disappointed look that was now on his face.

"Are you sure? We always stay here. We've been twice this year already."

"Of course, I will check for you. What name is it please?" She asked and beckoned him to follow her.

"Christina Hammond, with our two children, Ben and Natasha." Steve stood looking anxious as he watched the young waitress check the booking screen on the computer. She was already frowning as she scrolled down the list of the guests' names.

She looked up and shook her head. "I'm sorry, Mr. Hammond, but your wife hasn't got a reservation. As I said earlier, the wedding party has monopolised the whole building. We are completely full, I'm afraid."

Steve thanked her and walked back out onto the busy street. He tried Christina's phone again, but it was still switched off. He just hoped that Ben was playing something mindless on his. Steve jogged back to his car and was thankful that he hadn't caused a problem being parked where he was.

He now headed for the park, just on the off chance they might be there. He also knew there were usually parking spaces, especially at this time of the evening, then he could sit in comfort checking Ben's phone to find out where they were. There were surprisingly more cars than he had expected, but Christina's slate grey Dacia Jogger was not among them. He puffed out his cheeks in frustration and parked up.

He checked Christina's phone first. It was still switched off. His annoyance, however, quickly turned to joy when he saw that Ben still had his on. What concerned him now was the location. According to his son's phone, his wife was driving along the B3357, and she was somewhere between a place called Two Bridges and Dartmeet. "Where the hell are you going?" He said out loud, still staring at his mobile screen.

He absentmindedly looked up from his phone and suddenly realised just how dark it had become. According to his phone, it was eight thirty and now very gloomy outside. His heart raced at the thought of his wife out there somewhere, driving along a B road in the dark. He was also pretty sure that she had now ventured onto Dartmoor itself, with its steep dips and narrow twisty roads. He needed to catch her up and quickly.

The road out of Okehampton was fairly quick and wide. It started to change once he had turned left towards Two Bridge. He had to slow down, and the road was narrow in places. As soon as he went over the cattle grid, he knew he was now on Dartmoor, and very soon, his whole world was cast into darkness. He seemed to be completely alone. Just him against the night.

His satnav told him that Dartmeet was just up

ahead. Surely it wouldn't be long now before he would be reunited with Christina and the children. "Where the hell are you?" He muttered under his breath the exact moment a white-washed building close to the edge of the road seemed to spring up from nowhere.

Steve gripped the steering wheel firmly as the car gathered momentum down a small hill. He braked hard and swung the vehicle one way and then the other before suddenly careering over a narrow stone-arched bridge and back up the other side of the valley. He pulled over, applied the handbrake, and took a couple of deep breaths. He had been driving too quickly to get to Christina, and now he needed to compose himself before carrying on.

He checked his phone before carrying on. Christina's was, as he expected, still turned off, but now so was Ben's. He was now driving blind, and to make matters even worse, a fine drizzle of misty rain was blowing straight at him. His visibility was almost zero.

He didn't see the moving shape in front of him until the very last second. He slammed on his brakes, and the car skidded to the other side of the road. The Dartmoor pony didn't look back, but he showed Steve where Christina was parked. As he sat wondering how on earth he hadn't collided with the animal, he watched as it plodded over to a car parked in a large lay-by.

From where Steve sat, he couldn't see the colour or the registration, but his gut told him it was his wife. Still shaking from his near miss, he drove into the lay-by and pulled up alongside a slate grey Dacia. Regardless of the rain, he quickly got out of his car and tapped on the Dacia window. He saw the figure inside jump with fright.

Christina had to wipe away the condensation on the glass to be sure it really was Steve, even though Natasha was shouting, "Daddy." at the top of her voice. The car interior light came on, and Steve heard the familiar sound of the door lock click. And in an instant, he was sat in the passenger seat.

They both spoke the exact words at the same time. "What are you doing here?" Christina's voice sounded surprised and Steve's angry. In the dim light, he saw a little smile flash across his wife's face.

"I was getting away from you. The White Hart didn't have any rooms tonight, so I was heading back to Bristol."

"Not this way you weren't." He turned and put his arm over the back of the front seat as he spoke. Ben and Natasha both clutched at it and hung on. It was very uncomfortable, but he savoured the moment.

"I became disorientated because I was so angry at the thought of having to return home," Christina added quietly.

"Is life really that bad back there?" He asked, indicating to his children that he needed to move.

"Yes, Steve, it is, actually. It's unbearable. Even the kids will tell you that. You do nothing with them. You take me for granted on a daily basis. It's work, work, work with you, and nothing else."

"I've been an idiot."

"That's the understatement of the year." She fired back a little too quickly.

"Can we try again?" He asked, stretching his hand towards her. Christina looked down, and for what felt like forever to him, she eventually wrapped her fingers around his.

"If I can take that as a yes, we need to get out of here. Back the way we came is a hotel. It's called The Two Bridges. Just give me a minute." Steve reached for his mobile, googled the number, and pressed the buttons.

He smiled at his wife as he waited. "Hopefully, you can. My wife and I and our two young children are somewhat stranded out on the moors, just past Dartmeet. I was hoping you might have a room for the night?... Excellent. Thank you…Ten or fifteen minutes…..See you then. Bye."

"Please don't drive too quickly, Steve. I know you. I won't be able to keep up."

"I'm not leaving you now. Mine can stay here for the night. I'll drive yours."

"Over my dead body. This is my car. Now you're here. I feel a lot more confident. It just might take five minutes longer, that's all."

As Christina steadily manoeuvred onto the narrow road. Steve pulled an envelope from his pocket and passed it over to Ben. With the help of the interior light, he was able to read what his father had handed him.

"Mom. Mom. We're going to Disneyland in Paris." He yelled, showing the tickets to his sister. Steve asked them both to calm down while he explained to their mother. "I didn't go down the pub with the lads this afternoon, I went to the travel agents. I've been organising this for weeks. I was so sure of landing the Zimmerman contract, and my boss had promised me a break if we got it. So, we are going next week. If that's okay with you guys?" Steve turned the interior light off before pretending to put his hands over his ears because all three were screaming with delight.

ACE OF HEARTS

Inspired by: HOUSE OF THE RISING SUN
Performed by THE ANIMALS

As I quickly climbed aboard and pulled the sliding door closed, I realised how much the boxcar stank. It smelt like something or someone had died in here recently, but I had no choice. The train was already increasing its speed as I ran alongside the track. I had only a few seconds to clamber up and find out later where it was taking me. The only thing I knew for sure was we were heading east out of Galveston. I hoped to get as far as Jacksonville and be safe from the law.

The light faded fast as the evening drew in, and long shadows filled my surroundings. I took one last look at my pocket watch before deciding to try and get some sleep. I had been on the run all day and was utterly exhausted. My tatty denim jacket was a poor substitute for a pillow, but except for a few dollars in my back pocket, it was all I had.

Sleep was evading me. No matter how hard I tried, I couldn't get the sound of the screaming shop owner out of my head. It had all happened so quickly. She became hysterical when she caught me in the act. Then she began clutching her chest and staggering towards me. I wasn't even armed or threatening. I was just desperate for some food. I had grabbed two apples and a salami sausage on impulse, for heaven's sake. It's not as if I was holding up the whole goddam store.

The morning light was pouring through the wooden slats of the boxcar, and it was enough to rouse me. I also realised that the train had almost stopped moving. I rechecked my watch. It was nine-thirty, and I'd been asleep for twelve hours. As I stood up to investigate, the train juddered to a standstill, and I was thrown from one side to the other. I picked myself up and checked the back of my head, which was hurting like hell. My fingers revealed blood, but not very much. I had a minor cut, nothing more.

"Check down that way. We don't need any more drifters in Nola. We got more than our fair share. And be careful!" The gruff voice yelling outside quickly made me forget my aches and pains. I grabbed my jacket and carefully eased the sliding door open. I had chosen the right side of the track, and there was no one to be seen.

I jumped down as quietly as possible, but my shoes crunched loudly on the stone chippings, and I held my breath. No one came rushing and shouting between the boxcars to apprehend me, so I went undetected. The other good thing was I now knew my exact location. This was New Orleans, and I knew the locals called it Nola. Not quite Jacksonville and the Atlantic coast, but still well away from Galveston. I was happy, though. Having been here before, I knew a few places to hang out.

I hurried away from the freight train. Over my

shoulder, I realised someone had been caught, and it sounded like he was getting a hell of a beating. I kept moving. The quicker I could get out of the freight yard, the better. At least the rail workers were now preoccupied with pummelling the life out of someone. That's how it is. The civil war has been over for thirteen years, but the country is still trying to get back on its feet. Authorities don't want more people to worry about, more mouths to feed.

The last time I was here, some five years ago, I also came by train, but then I travelled in style, well, at least I had my own seat for the journey. I quickly got my bearings and headed south down to the river. I had an idea of how to disappear. Sometimes being aboard a Mississippi steamer, you can easily just blend in, but first, I had things to do.

The waterfront was heaving with people, mules and cargo. There seemed to be dozens of steamboats moored and thousands upon thousands of cotton bales stacked everywhere. It was so easy for me to be invisible among the workers. I did nothing other than walk around as though I belonged there. No one paid me a second glance, and everything I was looking for was waiting for me.

Within ten minutes, I had a waistcoat, a jacket and a new cap, all courtesy of two white foremen, who had stripped down to open-necked shirts and were squaring up to each other over an argument about labour. Whilst they sorted out their differences, I sorted out their clothing. Now all I needed was a clean shirt and somewhere to scrub up, and I knew just the place.

I headed away from the busy river and made my way to Basin Street. I walked towards the old cemetery before turning down a side street. As far as bordello houses go, The Cats Whiskers, tucked away behind a small shop front, wasn't the city's most prominent or best establishment. But Winnie, the owner, and I were old friends. I helped her out on my last visit when a nasty customer was slapping one of her favourite girls around. She had said I was always welcome back, and now I was about to accept her invitation.

It's not often you get the chance to have two attractive young ladies scrubbing your back and washing your legs, so I lay back and made the most of the situation. They had both produced warm towels with the offer to dry me afterwards, but there were some jobs that I preferred to do myself, which included shaving. I would never trust anyone to hold a razor to my throat.

Now lying in bed with my two ladies still in attendance, being spoon-fed shrimp, chicken, and sausage mixed with peppers and rice, was my idea of heaven. Especially when I knew what the second course was going to be. I could hardly wait, but I did, letting food and a soft, warm bed take over.

By morning, Winnie had found me a fresh white shirt and a new pair of trousers. Plus, a rather fancy silk cravat. I looked the business, a total transformation from yesterday. Winnie was also brave enough to go one step further and trust me with some of her hard-earned money. Which meant, in total, I had just over one hundred dollars, not a lot but enough to get me started. I just needed to get aboard one of those steamboats.

Three kisses later, I was walking back down

to the Mississippi river with, I have to admit, a slight swagger. I now looked like a gentleman, complete with an ebony walking cane, courtesy of some male visitor who walked into The Cats Whiskers hobbling but left with such new vigour that he had left it behind. Now all I had to do, was remember my new gentlemanly role and try hard to fulfil it.

It wasn't hard finding the right steamer. I only had to wander slowly up and down a couple of times before seeing enough to know which one to choose. What's more, she was ready to sail. I paid for the cheapest cabin I could. I didn't see the point in wasting good money on a bed I wasn't planning to use very much. I wanted my time on here to be short and sweet. Knowing when to call it a day is the secret to success.

I spent the first couple of hours watching, moving slowly around the smoky, tobacco-filled stateroom from one table to another, looking over shoulders, weighing up the opposition. I quickly found my mark, and now I just had to wait until one of the players had run out of money or had had enough for the night. Like my father before me, I knew who and when to strike. It was all down to timing.

I made a point of staying away from the bar and especially the barmaids, who always offered more than just waitress service. I needed a clear head, so I walked around with a lemon-flavoured sarsaparilla for most of the evening, with little intention of drinking it. I would celebrate with a good bottle of whiskey later.

I heard the loud voices and headed straight for the table, and it looked as if I was about to get my chance. A very drunk, well-dressed man was being escorted to the door. I arrived before anyone else and placed my hand on the back of the now vacant chair.

"Gentleman, may I join you? It seems someone has had enough for the night." I looked across the room and watched as two of his friends tried their best to hold him up.

"Well, he's had enough liquor. That's for sure." The card player sitting directly opposite me growled as he scooped up his winnings. "Sit, but that aint no lucky chair. Certainly not for him anyway." He laughed loudly at his own joke as he tidied up his money.

"The name's Boyd, John Boyd," I said, looking around the table. The man opposite, the one clearly having the better night regarding the cards, replied first. "Henry Chandler. " I noticed the fresh-faced young man on my right straighten when Chandler said his name.

"Eddie Harper." He replied, nodding at me and smiling before looking back at Chandler. It made me wonder if they were in this together, playing as a team. Even though they seemed complete opposites. Chandler was rough and ready in appearance, probably about forty years of age. Whilst Harper looked about eighteen, although I guessed he was nearer twenty-five, twenty-six. The fourth man sat with us eventually confirmed his name as Frank and left it at that.

I quickly changed my mind about Chandler and Harper being in cahoots with each other. Eddie Harper was no card player. He was all fingers and thumbs when dealing and couldn't shuffle a deck to save his life. But something was going on around this table. I just didn't know what that was at the moment.

My hundred-dollar stake quickly grew. I was getting some juicy cards, but not I noticed when Chandler was dealing. When he dealt, he usually won. He was cheating, but I hadn't caught him yet, which meant he was good. I was better, of course, and not as greedy as him. Winning slowly may take longer, but it doesn't attract attention. He was making it too obvious, at least to me, he was. The other two seemed oblivious to the fact.

I was now aware of people standing over our shoulders. Our table was causing a lot of interest, mainly because Chandler made such a loud statement every time he took the pot and raked the money back into his growing pile. I was getting tired of his antics, as was Eddie Harper. Twice now, I had seen him fidget in his chair as if he was going to call Chandler out and question his honesty.

Just after midnight Frank, the man with no surname left the three of us to it. My guess was he had lost about three hundred dollars, of which Chandler and I seemed to have an equal share. I had well over four hundred dollars in front of me, and Henry Chandler had nearer six. Babyface Eddie was holding his own for someone I suspected was not used to playing for such high stakes. The time felt right for me to strike. I just needed to be careful and watchful of Chandler.

An hour later, and it was all very one-sided. We were playing the end game. Eddie had stacked and left Chandler and me to fight it out. There was a buzz of excitement around the table. Those that hadn't drifted off to bed were now standing in little groups behind the pair of us. I called him out and watched as he lay his cards down one at a time, taking the opportunity to tell me each card as if I couldn't read.

"Two of diamonds, four of diamonds, six of diamonds, seven of diamonds, and last but not least, the ten of diamonds. A nice red flush." He smirked at me as he sat back in his chair. I nodded but kept my face straight. I had called him, so he thought I probably didn't have much on offer. The truth was, I was tired, and I needed my bed. There was always tomorrow.

"Three aces." I hesitated just long enough to watch him eagerly stretch forward. "Plus two jacks. A full house, I believe, Mr. Chandler?" His eyes widened, and his mouth became distorted. I was a little nervous. I had probably pushed him too far. There was also a lot of money in the middle of that table.

As I scooped it all towards me, I saw young Eddie moving slightly in his chair, but Chandler was already standing up. "You're either a lucky son of a bitch, or a cheat, Mr. Boyd." I stayed as relaxed as I could.

"I think it was just my evening tonight. I'll be here tomorrow if you care to sit in?" Chandler hesitated, but it was enough to calm the situation down. I looked up at him as I stacked my newly earned money and watched his face. He rubbed his chin. He was overacting. He was trying to give us the impression that he was thinking things through when he already had a plan.

"How much you reckon you got there?" He asked, placing both hands on the table and leaning into my face. I had already counted some of my winnings, so I had a fair idea.

"A thousand, maybe twelve hundred dollars." I sat up as if I was interested in hearing him out.

"How's about you take a thousand and place it in the middle of the table, and let's see how much of a gambler you really are?"

"What are you proposing, Mr. Chandler?" I asked, but not doing as he requested. He straightened up and pulled a leather pouch from an inside jacket pocket. He held it up for me to see, bouncing it in his palm. "This here is my reserve." He tossed it across to Eddie, who knew his job without being asked. He pulled the edges of the pouch open and looked inside. Eddie nodded to me that it was indeed enough. "My proposal, as you so put it, is that I can cut the ace of hearts in one go."

I smiled to myself. No one makes that statement unless they know they can do it, and he certainly didn't have the ace of hearts up his sleeve. It was one of the cards I had held with my full house. Nevertheless, I wanted to be sure of the rules.

"Correct me if I am wrong, Mr. Chandler, but you predict that you can cut the ace of hearts with just one attempt?" Henry Chandler nodded and smiled. He was confident, too confident for my liking. I turned to Eddie and indicated that he put the pouch in the centre of the table. I, in turn, counted out a thousand dollars

Eddie unceremoniously tipped the contents of the pouch onto the table, and gold coins were suddenly everywhere. Wheeling and spinning in all directions. I left it to him to gather them all together. My heart raced at the sight of so much money, but it wasn't mine yet.

Chandler handed the deck to Eddie and asked him to shuffle. He was so amateurish and nervous that they spilled from his hands twice before he gave them to me. I checked with Henry Chandler, that he had no objection that I got on with it before giving the pack the shuffling of their lives. When finished, I placed the deck in the middle of the table and rested my hand's palm down.

Everyone in the stateroom was now gathered around our table. There were many mumblings as people told others what was happening. Then the room fell silent, and I suspected people were anxiously holding their breath. "One cut and one cut only," I confirmed. Chandler nodded, and the sneer was back on his face.

His hand moved so quickly that I only saw a glint of something shiny before the knife he now had in his hand was thrust down straight through the deck of cards. Everyone in the room heard the loud thud as the blade made contact with the table.

"I believe I have just cut the ace of hearts." He roared, releasing the knife and raising his arms aloft in triumph. People standing close were slapping him on the back and saying *well done, bravo*. I pinched my lips together and waited until he was back, looking down at me. Then I slowly raised my right hand and revealed the ace of hearts resting in my palm.

He took a lunge and swung his fist in my direction. I leaned back and felt the draught of his hand as it missed my face by inches. I pushed the chair back and stood. In the time it took, Chandler had pulled his knife from the cards and hurled it straight at me. It lodged in my shoulder, and I staggered off balance, trying to pull it out at the same time.

It was then that I saw Eddie Harper move. He pulled a small gun from his boot, cocked it, and pointed straight at Chandler's head. "Pinkerton Detective Agency. I'm agent Harper, and I'm arresting you for attempted murder. Do not move, or I promise I will pull the trigger without hesitation." Chandler stood stock still, hardly daring to breathe.

"Will someone please fetch the captain? I want this man in irons immediately." In the foray, no one questioned the young, fresh-faced man, as everything and everyone in the room stood still. Agent Harper pulled a metal badge from his inside pocket and flashed it for all to see. Someone standing close confirmed he was indeed from the Pinkerton Agency.

I finally got my shot of whiskey after the stateroom was cleared, and Chandler was deep in the bowels of the paddle steamer chained to the wall in a storage room. Eddie was sitting next to me as we raised our glasses.

"Thank you for that, Mr. Harper. It was my lucky day that you were on board." Eddie shook his head. "It wasn't luck, John. I've been shadowing Henry Chandler for over three weeks now." He saw my puzzled look. "He robbed a bank back in Albuquerque. Knifed the manager in the process. Which also means you might not be as rich as you think."

"You mean…"

"I'm afraid so. The Albuquerque National Bank is going to want their money back. All five hundred dollars of it." He smiled and winked and waited for me to fall in.

SCRAMBLED LOVE

Inspired by: YESTERDAY
Performed by THE BEATLES

Tuesday, February the fourteenth, for the romantics, Valentine's Day. For me, possibly the worst day of my life. It had all started so well, or so I thought. Maxine was still in bed, and I knew I needed to make an effort. We had had words last night, nothing very serious, but she had made her point and slept the whole night with her back to me and the duvet pulled up tight beneath her chin.

So, my grand gesture had been to make breakfast, her favourite, scrambled eggs with a sprinkling of cayenne pepper, French toast, and a mug of strong black coffee. I even found some red coloured card and cut out a large heart shape, and used it as a place mat on the breakfast tray. It looked lovely, again, that was only my opinion, but I was thrilled with the result.

I placed the tray on the bedside table and told her it was there. I could tell she was feigning sleep, but I accepted that perhaps she still wasn't in the right frame of mind to talk to me. She needed to do things at her own speed, in her own time. Maxine had always been that way, and it was something that I just had to accept.

The rest of the day, nothing seemed to improve. I felt so far away at work and wanted to be near her. To make matters worse, she didn't answer any of my calls. I sent her text messages asking how she was feeling and begging her to speak to me. She knew we had a reservation at a well-known and, of course, expensive restaurant. What Maxine didn't know was I had important things that I wanted to say to her. Some life-changing things.

When I arrived home, Maxine wasn't there. There was no note, but the tray of untouched scrambled eggs, toast, and coffee on the kitchen table told me everything. The house was so quiet, but it was screaming at me in my head. I took the stairs two at a time and dashed into the bedroom. It was in complete disarray. There were clothes scattered everywhere. Most were mine, and a few were hers, but the truth was, the wardrobes were empty. I slumped back on the bed as tears filled my eyes. She had gone, she really had gone.

After what felt like a lifetime, I regained enough composure to call Emma. She was Maxine's best friend and her life-long confidante, who was always there for her when she had a problem, such as now. But I guessed she would be hard work and remain tight-lipped.

We talked briefly, and I was right. She lied to me the whole time. She knew precisely where Maxine was. I could almost visualise the two of them sitting, holding hands, giggling as Emma spoke with me. Telling me too quickly that she wasn't there, so don't bother calling around.

Wednesday the fifteenth, and I've called in sick. Some of my work colleagues will wrongly assume that I'm not there because I over-enjoyed Valentine's night, but they would be so wrong. In the cold light of day, I should probably have done more, but I had convinced myself that she was just punishing me and would come home when she was ready. I sat up most of the night texting Maxine, even though I knew it was futile, but sleep doesn't come easy with a scrambled brain. So, trying to do something positive seemed better than over-engaging with the vodka bottle that had been at my side throughout the whole night.

I knew Emma was the key to this. If I was wrong, and Maxine wasn't there, then at least she would know where she was. My biggest problem was that Emma and I had form. We went out together for just over a year, and then she introduced me to Maxine, and everything for me changed.

I moved back into the small house I had been renting out, and Maxine moved in with me. Emma, of course, didn't take it very well. She tried everything to get me to return, but I was head over heels in love with Maxine. Throughout this upheaval, the two of them remained best friends. How that works in a woman's mind, I have no idea. I did know that Emma wouldn't be very cooperative with me, that was for sure.

Having parked away from the house, I checked some of the side streets to see if Maxine had left her Mini Cooper discreetly out of sight. It was nowhere to be seen. Perhaps she wasn't here after all. But I still needed to be sure, and the only way to achieve that was to ring Emma's front doorbell.

Memories came flooding back as I walked up the concrete steps that led to her Victorian terraced house.

I stood inside the open porch staring at the two ornate lead-lined window panels. I could picture Emma walking down the hall, checking her appearance as she always did in the mirror before opening the door. Then she was there, moving gracefully towards me. I could see her distorted silhouette through the various coloured shapes.

The door swung open. "I guessed as much. She's not here. You're wasting your time." Emma batted her eyes and gave me a wry smile.

"May I come in anyway?" I asked nervously.

"Nope. I've much better things to do with my mornings." She stretched an arm across the opening and leaned on the doorjamb, clearly communicating her intentions.

"I want ten minutes of your time, not the whole fricking morning."

"Oh, all of a sudden, you have time for me. Well, that is rich!" Emma had straightened up, stepped over the threshold, and was right in my face.

"Morning Emma." A female voice called out from the street. I turned and looked at the elderly lady standing at the gate. "More company. Gosh, you are busy today."

"Morning, Mrs. Higgins." I turned back to Emma and gave her a knowing smile. She raised both her hands in surrender. "Okay, you win. Ten minutes, that's all."

As we walked into the large front room, I was pleased to see the oil painting I had given her still hanging above the mantlepiece. I pointed to it. "I never thought you liked it that much?"

"Are you here to discuss cheap works of art? Or Maxine?" She scowled, pointing for me to sit on the sofa while she sat in the armchair directly opposite.

"So, she is here?" I dived straight in. I clearly wasn't going to be offered a coffee, and I only had ten minutes.

"Nope, she was, and now she isn't." Emma sat back and crossed her long slender legs, and the wry smile was back on her face.

"God, this is going to be hard work."

"What were you expecting?" She countered. "Less than a year ago, you were living here under my roof, telling me that you were deeply in love with me. How meeting me had changed your life. Letting me introduce you to my circle of friends, of which Maxine was one. And then, when you had finished with me, you simply cast me aside and took up with one of my best friends."

She was right, of course, but it wasn't that straightforward. "But you forgave Maxine and not me?"

"I was in love with you. But I didn't listen to those around me. Telling me that I was being used. Setting you up with your own art studio, using my influential friends and power to help promote your paintings." My eyes went straight to the chimney breast. I had always thought of that painting as genuinely being my best.

"I hear you don't even paint these days?" I shrugged the comment away. Desperate to change the subject. My time was running out, and I had no doubt that Emma would show me the door in exactly ten minutes.

"So, if Maxine isn't here now, where is she?" I asked, leaning forward, pleading with my eyes.

"I promised her that I wouldn't tell you. In fact, I told her you wouldn't get past the bloody front door."

"But here I am, and I'm desperate, Em. I was going to ask her to marry me. I had the ring and everything!" Emma was already agreeing with me, nodding her head as I spoke.

"I know, she told me." I sat back dumbfounded. Emma could see my confused state.

"She found the ring, along with your little speech. It frightened the shit out of her. She isn't ready to settle down. She has plans of her own. She wants to see the world. Thailand, Japan, China even. Not be stuck here with…."

"Me!" I finished her sentence for her. "I thought she felt the same as I did." I continued quickly, looking straight at Emma. "I thought we were right for each other. Obviously not. All this time, and I had it wrong."

Emma uncrossed her legs and moved to the sofa next to me. She perched on the edge of the black leather seat, placed her warm hand on top of mine, and gently rubbed the back of my hand and fingers. It felt nice, but it was also very unnerving.

"I gave you so much, Ryan, and I asked for so little in return." Her soothing fingers were working wonders to calm my pulse rate, but what a strange remark to make. Why has this suddenly become about her? I soon found out.

"We seem to have the classic eternal triangle going on here." Emma paused as she thought her following words through carefully. "Let's see how it works. I love you passionately, always have, and always will, but you don't love me. You love Maxine, but she doesn't seem to love you." She paused, and that smile was back. "Aah, yes, the best piece of the triangle, and the most important bit, Maxine loves me." I felt my jaw drop open. What the hell had I just been told?

"Maxine loves you?" I gasped, pulling my hand away. Emma nodded, and the smile broadened. "Intensely. With all her body and soul, the poor girl. She is completely obsessed with me." Emma, by now, was almost laughing in my face.

"But…...you don't love her?" I questioned, already knowing I didn't need to hear the answer.

"No, Ryan, not at all. Not one teeny weenie bit. But, if I can't have you, then certainly someone I know can't have you either."

"How has this all happened so quickly?" I asked, standing and moving into the middle of the room. My head was reeling, and my emotions were completely off the scale.

"It hasn't been quick, Ryan. It's taken time. About three months of careful planning, knowing when to invite her over. Talking to her and pointing out a few of your manly faults, some grossly exaggerated and a few wildly untrue, of course. But she does seem to be so easily led. I even told her that I thought you were gay. Thus planting the idea into her head before I made my move on her." Emma stood up and stepped close to me, which was rather brave because I had to control myself from slapping her across her smug smiley face.

"How could you be so cruel and nasty?" I

looked her straight in the eyes and gritted my teeth, the anger showing on my face. She laughed out loud. "You look so childlike when you are cross as if you were about to cry. You've lost her, Ryan. I've taken Maxine from you. What's more, we're going away later this week to all the places she has dreamed of."

"What's going on?" The voice from the doorway made us both turn around. Maxine was standing there, lowering a shopping bag to the floor. Emma was quicker to react than I was.

"Maxie, you're back. He just barged his way in." Emma gushed, opening her arms and walking briskly towards her.

"I didn't, Maxine. She allowed me ten minutes to talk." I countered. Emma stopped and turned to face me.

"Maybe I did, but your time is up, so leave now." She demanded, pointing towards the bay window and the world outside. She was put in her place as soon as she turned back to Maxine with her arms extended once more.

"Stay there, Emma. I'm still digesting what I've been hearing." Maxine looked angry and pointed an accusing finger at her. How long had she been there standing in the hall? I certainly didn't hear the front door open or close. Was everything about to change? Twenty-four hours ago, my world had seemingly collapsed into a black hole, but now there might be a small chink of light breaking through. It all depended on Maxine.

"Maxie, whatever you heard or thought you heard. It was just my way of protecting you from him." Emma sounded desperate. Her voice was raised but more in panic than anger. We both watched

Maxine standing there, shaking her head.

"No, Emma, you're lying now as you have done from the start. You've been slowly poisoning me, trying to turn me against him. And it almost worked. You very nearly convinced me." She paused, hesitating to carry on, but thankfully, she did.

"My god, I've been so stupid." She looked straight at me when she spoke, and tears formed in her eyes. I smiled and nodded that it was okay. Thankfully she fully understood what I was inferring and ran past Emma and threw her arm around my neck. We kissed long and hard to the sound of Emma screaming. "NOoo…..." At the top of her lungs.

HIS FINAL WORDS

Inspired by: HALLELUJAH
Performed by Leonard Cohen

Michael fidgeted uncomfortably on the hard wooden chair and was feeling uneasy about the whole experience, trying to convince himself that he was doing the right thing sitting there. It had taken him nearly half an hour of pacing up and down outside the church to get this far. He had to force himself to enter the house of God. He knew that this was the end of the road for him. Everything hinged on what took place inside these hallowed walls. Now he had walked through those doors. There was no turning back.

He checked his watch, he had been waiting ten minutes already, and it felt like a lifetime. It was proving to be very traumatic. Even the simple placement of the chairs was causing him concern. They were in a single line adjacent to the back wall, meaning that everyone who entered could see him and would know why he was there. He was also the only male sitting there silently, waiting his turn.

He hadn't expected a queue. Was everyone as desperate as he was to confess their sins? It would seem so. Perhaps everyone had something to confess.

If so, why wasn't the whole world repenting along with him?

Eventually, it was his turn, and his moment had arrived. He stepped nervously into the wooden cubicle and sat on the smooth, polished seat. The noise of a sliding door opening close to his face made him jump. He glanced towards it and saw the figure of a priest, then quickly turned his head away.

"Forgive me, Father, for I have sinned." *Wasn't that what everyone said?* He had never been to a confessional before. The truth was he had hardly ever stepped inside a church. As a lad, he had always skipped Sunday school to go fishing or hang around with the older boys outside the local coffee bar, learning about life on the street.

"Go on, my son. God and I are listening as one." The words were so icy that Michael felt goosebumps rise on his arms, and he shivered. He was tempted to stand up and leave, throw back the thick heavy purple curtain, and flee through the church doors. Anything seemed better than feeling trapped inside this oak-carved box.

"I need your guidance, father. I need to repent my love for a woman."

"I am not here to guide you, my son. I am here to listen, and when you are finished, I will judge. But I need to hear your confession in full." Michael had hoped that the priest would be more understanding. He had spent hours trying to get his head around his dire situation. He had come to the church out of desperation because he needed someone to listen to him, help, and advise him.

"I loved her so much. I worshipped the ground that she walked on. I tried so hard to tell her how much I loved her, but she never listened. I wrote poetry for her, but she didn't read my words. Others did and were blown away by my verses of love. Before she came into my life, I saw who I wished, and I wined and dined with who I wanted. Women flocked to me. I was the one, but they came and went to order, for I was in charge of my own destiny. Then Dee entered my life. I gave her the best of everything, but nothing moved her. She was never overly impressed. Yet throughout our affair, I was at her mercy, her beck and call. Whatever she asked for, I gave it to her. Whatever she did to me, I accepted my fate. She controlled me and stopped me from seeing other women. She took away all my power with a simple kiss and, all the time, pretending to believe me when I said that I only loved her."

Michael paused. Recalling how much he loved her and how it was more painful than he had ever imagined. Something deep inside was telling him to leave. Forget this stupid idea of confessing his love for a woman who had mistreated and belittled him. He wasn't even sure how much detail he would now divulge to the faceless priest sitting on the other side of the ornately decorated screen.

"If you wish to continue, my son, I am here. I am listening." The soft voice pricked at his conscience. Michael took a deep breath and carried on.

"We used to be so close, and there were times when she would spend hours explaining how she felt inside, confessing everything to me as I am now to you, and for that, I loved her even more. But at the end of the day, we just hurt each other. Ours was a painful love, and it broke my heart." As he spoke, he could picture the scene in his head.

Dee was standing there, her suitcase on one side and a large duffle bag on the other. He remembered protesting that it was nearly midnight and still raining outside. That leaving now was silly. *Stay at least until the morning. Surely that makes sense?* Seeing her standing in front of him smiling, almost taunting him, had suddenly made him feel angry. He clenched his fists as he stared back at her.

He thought about the following morning. He had never been so drunk in his life, and all because the only woman he ever really loved had gone. Begging her to stay, and offering her money, were both stupid ideas. She was never going to say yes. She was much too stubborn for that. In the end, her demands were all too much. He had little choice, and now she was gone forever.

"There was no hope for us, father. I found it so hard to understand her. We were no longer good together, even though I had never loved anyone like her. I couldn't go on living with her." Michael's urge to get up and run had returned, but he needed to see this through to the finish.

"The end for me is here, father. I couldn't live with her, yet I couldn't live without her. I had to make a choice. May the Lord forgive me for what I have done." Michael felt tears forming in his eyes. He sat back, rested his weary head against the back panel of the confessional box, and closed his eyes.

"And what exactly is that, my son?" Michael opened his eyes and leaned forward. He felt it was now or never and ran his tongue over his dry lips. "It pains me to say it out loud, father. When you love someone as much as I loved Dee, accepting the truth is hard to bear, even when you know the truth."

The priest shuffled on his bench and sat closer to the dividing screen as he sensed the atmosphere in the cubicle change. "Take your time, my son. You will feel all the better for telling me." Michael knew that he couldn't say anymore. He had confessed his love for this woman. That would have to be enough. People would have to judge him by that and that alone when they found her and what he had done. Without another word, he took the gun out of his pocket and placed the cold steel barrel against his temple.

IN PLAIN SIGHT

Inspired by: EVERY BREATH YOU TAKE
Performed by THE POLICE

Georgina was pleased with her student flat. It was small but compact, and the view of the park from the window was stunning. It was a vast improvement from her last place, which overlooked the railway line, and the litter-strewn embankment. What's more, this place wasn't going to shudder and rattle every time a speeding express train shot through. Also, this flat was within walking distance of the university, and there was no steep hill to climb.

Desmond, or Des as he liked to be called, bothered her slightly when he initially showed her around. He seemed like an oddball, with long straight hair down to his shoulders, a little goatee beard, and sunken cheeks. All of which seemed to emphasise his long, pointed nose. He gave her the creeps, and he was undoubtedly in need of a hot shower.

But the rent was affordable, and she could keep herself to herself and stay well away from his downstairs room. She didn't know much more about him except his father, who lived permanently in France, had converted the large house into flats. So, she was answerable to him.

Georgina had settled quickly into her new

abode. Everything had been unpacked and put away, and the water had been nice and hot after her shower. Now, she wanted to investigate the park across the road. It was a lovely sunny afternoon, and she thought the fresh air would do her good. She was halfway down the stairs when Desmond opened his door and stood in her way.

"Hi, Georgina. Everything up there okay?" He asked, pulling down on his goatee with a finger and thumb. Georgina smiled and nodded. She really didn't want to get into a discussion with him. She wanted to be outside but didn't want to antagonise him.

"Yes, it's lovely. Thank you, Desmond.

"Des. Please call me Des. After all, we do share a house together." He grinned, and Georgina cringed at the thought as she eased her way past him.

"Of course, you told me that last week when I came to view." She had already said too much. Desmond scurried along the red-tiled floor of the hall and arrived at the front door first. He turned the yale lock and pulled on it. The open door allowed the sun to flood the house and bathe them in its warmth.

"Bye," Georgina called over her shoulder, closing her eyes with relief as she strode down the narrow garden path. As she placed her hand on the wrought iron gate, she knew he was still standing watching her. She could feel his eyes on the back of her head. She knew that going to the park was no longer a good idea. If she went there, he would follow her. Of that, she was sure. "Forget the park and explore the surrounding area." She muttered under her breath, turning to the left and marching down the street.

Georgina's flat was empty, but he knew that. He just wanted a quick view around, check that everything was in working order. He sat and looked at all four screens, one after the other. The first one was of little interest. The camera angle covered the flat door and the stairs. He knew that the first was working okay. He had used it to watch her leave and lock her door. Camera two covered the main room and kitchen area, but three and four excited him the most. The bedroom and the bathroom.

He zoomed in on the bed. "Oh, that is sweet. You have a cuddly panda on your pillow," he mocked and laughed. "Hurry back to me, Georgina. I can't wait to see you." As he checked the final screen in the bathroom, the picture flickered off and on before disappearing altogether. His mood changed instantly. "Damn and blast you, Georgina. The sign in the bathroom clearly says, *please turn on the extractor fan before showering.* Now you've gone and got moisture in the works." He slammed his fist hard down on the desktop in frustration.

As Georgina slowly walked back towards her lodgings, she couldn't help feeling anxious. She had no real reason to. It was just something about her landlord, Desmond, that she found intimidating. But she could handle herself. That much was certain. She had never used her karate skills in anger, but she knew she wouldn't hesitate if he gave her any trouble.

As she approached the gate leading up to the house, she glanced across the road towards the park. In the distance, she could see Desmond looking left and right as he strolled along the path in her direction. Georgina hurried. She wanted to get inside before he spotted her.

She fiddled with the key, but it wouldn't go into the lock. Her fumbling made it slip through her fingers, and by the time she had picked it up, she could hear Desmond calling for her to wait. She didn't turn around and pretended not to hear him, pushed the key hard into the lock, and turned it. Within seconds, she was through the front door and running up the stairs.

Once inside, she slumped against the closed door and sighed with relief. She also gave herself a good talking to. "Get a grip, Georgie. This is all in your head. He hasn't done anything for you to react like this. He's your landlord and you need to be a bit friendlier." She laughed at her silliness, went into the kitchen area, and put the kettle on. "A strong coffee is what you need." She chirped, feeling more cheerful as she spooned the aromatic granules into her favourite mug.

She heard the front door slam, and it jarred her nerves, she assumed it was Desmond, and he wasn't thrilled. She prayed he wouldn't come to her room and knock on the door. She certainly couldn't pretend she wasn't in. He had already seen her entering the house. Georgina waited and found she was almost holding her breath in anticipation. After several minutes, she decided that he had gone straight to his own room, making her blow out her cheeks in relief.

Georgina had tossed and turned all night, she had woken up several times, once to go to the bathroom, and the second time, for reasons best known to herself, she checked the security chain on the front door. In her semi-conscious state, she hadn't remembered that she had put it on much earlier in the afternoon when she was trying to avoid Desmond.

By midday, she had cleaned the bathroom from top to bottom and concentrated on the kitchen area. The knock on her door made her jump. She turned quickly and just stood staring at it. It was as if she had some magical powers to make whoever it was standing on the other side suddenly disappear.

There was a second knock, this time louder. "Georgie, are you there? It's Samantha." Georgina dropped her wet cloth in the sink and ran to the door. The second that it was open, she wrapped her arms around her friend. "I'm sorry, Sam, I completely forgot you were coming today, and it can't be lunchtime already?"

"It certainly is. Well, are you going to show me around your beautiful palace or not?" Georgina smiled at her friend's remark. Less than a month ago, she made the flippant remark that anything new would be like a mansion compared to the hovel she was in, down by the railway line. Georgina watched as Samantha looked at everything before stepping into her bedroom.

"Oh my, a king-sized bed all to yourself." She quipped, smiling and widening her hazel brown eyes, before bouncing up and down on the edge. "Very nice, very nice indeed." As she stood up, she saw the clock on the wall and looked closer. "This, however, is a little bit tacky. It's very retro. All these shiny pointed shards sticking out by the numbers. Yak."

Desmond shot back in his chair as the dark brown eyeball almost popped out through the screen.

"Jesus, lady, how close do you need to get." He huffed, trying to regain his composure. Then as if Samantha had heard him, she stepped away from the clock and faced her friend. "I am joking with you, Georgie. It's all very nice." Georgina nodded that she understood. "As I said, it's better than before. But anything would be. I hated living down there."

"So, are we eating in or going out? If we go out, it's my treat. I know you poor students don't have two pennies to rub together." Samantha teased her friend. It was always the same between them. Georgina wanted to go to university and study for a degree in architecture, while Samantha wanted nothing more than to work in an office and earn some real money.

"There's a nice little bistro just around the corner. I spotted it yesterday while exploring the area." Georgina was already walking towards the door, leaving her friend in her wake. "Hold on, speedy." Georgina stopped and looked back. "French or Italian?" Samantha asked, waving her on. They both laughed, especially when Georgina replied, "Spanish."

From the outside, the bistro looked small and cramped, but after hesitating for a few seconds, they stepped inside and were amazed at how much room there really was. It just seemed to go on forever. There were quiet corners, dazzling bright areas, and even a piano. They were quickly shown to a table, presented with menus, and offered drinks. Georgina checked with Samantha before she ordered a glass of prosecco. She knew her friend was driving and would have sparkling water.

After ordering their food and being presented

with their drinks, they both sat chatting, keeping up with the gossip, checking if any boyfriends were on the horizon. When that was all done asking about work.

"So, what's new in the housing market?" She asked, sipping at her wine. Samantha nodded and smiled. "Well, we are still finding good, cheap accommodation for struggling would-be architects." Her smile broadened, and she raised her glass of water in salute.

"I can never thank you enough for that. The student housing association said there was nothing available nearer to the university, but you have found me the perfect affordable place ever."

"My pleasure Georgie." She replied just as their food arrived. "This looks yummy. Well done. A good find." They tucked into crispy fried calamari and coconut chicken in a turmeric curry. Taking it in turns to delve into each other's dishes, they nodded with approval at every mouthful.

"Do you know that chap over there, Georgie?" Samantha asked, wiping the corners of her mouth with her napkin and looking over near the bar. Before Georgina could look, the figure turned and walked out of the bistro door. "Don't bother he's gone now. It's just that he kept staring over in our direction before suddenly leaving." Georgina felt her heart sink, she needed to ask Samantha what he looked like, but she sensed that she already knew the answer.

"Did he have long hair, a goatee beard, and a long, pointed nose?"

"You do have a boyfriend." Samantha laughed before seeing her friend's pained look.

"Georgie, what is it? What's the matter?" Samantha stretched her hand across the table, and Georgina accepted it and squeezed hard.

"I think it was Desmond, my landlord, who is certainly not my boyfriend. There is something quite unnerving about him, although, in fairness, he hasn't done or said anything to me, really. He just seems to be around all the time, watching me. Oh, I don't know, Sammy. It could just be me. What with the moving and all that."

"You poor thing. Let's change the subject and check out the desserts?" Georgina nodded and returned a weak smile, which didn't go unnoticed by her friend.

Samantha had walked back to the house with Georgina, and they had kissed and hugged, promising each other to stay in touch. Now Georgina was back in her room, sitting with her laptop, revising her notes before tomorrow's lecture. But for whatever reason, she couldn't concentrate. Other little things were whirring around in her head. So, she decided to take a shower. Standing under hot water and letting the warmth penetrate her body worked every time.

"Nice Georgina, very nice indeed. And you remembered to turn the extractor fan on, clever girl, a perfect picture." Desmond smiled as he stared at his screen and pressed the record button. He was happier now, back at home. His day had been full of frustration. He had tried to follow Georgina earlier when she went for a walkabout. But he lost her and doubled back, thinking that maybe she was really going to the park. But he couldn't find her there, and then she ignored him when he called out as she entered the house. He also hadn't liked how Georgina's friend looked at him in the bistro.

Samantha had driven home with a picture of Georgina in her head, and she wasn't happy with the image she saw. Her friend was emotionally upset with this Desmond character, and she was having none of that. Their friendship went a long way back, and she trusted Georgina's instincts.

After arriving in the office on Monday morning, it took Samantha less than ten minutes to find what she needed. She quickly punched in the numbers.

"Good morning. Is Rob there, please?" She sat and waited, but not for long.

"Rob, hi, it's Samantha from Stewart and Summers…. I'm well, thank you, and you?…. Glad to hear it. Listen, Rob, you know that rental house we took from you earlier this year?…. The one in Copeland Road, up by the university…." Samantha laughed, listening to Rob Mathews defending the fact that the company she worked for had taken another one of his clients.

She stopped laughing very quickly. "You are joking, right!" She hurriedly spread the sheets of paper she had taken from the filing cabinet across her desk, looking for the right one. "It says here that your client, Mr D. Whitlock wanted to change to us because he didn't think that you were doing enough for him. That you weren't finding him the right clientele."

Samantha could feel her heart pounding. She had been on annual leave when he walked into their office and gave her colleague all of his details. Now she was finding out from Rob Mathews that there was much more to this than met the eye.

"To be clear here, Rob. You're telling me that you dropped Mr Whitlock because one of your clients complained about his behaviour and that she thought he was spying on her?.... So, why didn't you call the authorities?.... What, and they did nothing?" Samantha was becoming more and more concerned as the conversation progressed.

"So, Pascal went back to France for family reasons, and as far as you know, they didn't do a follow-up. Bloody marvellous.... No, it's okay, honest. It's just that my best friend is currently staying there, and I arranged it all for her.... Rob, it's not your fault. It's the police that are at fault here. Perhaps there was a breakdown in communications.... Yes, Cheers, Rob.... Of course, I'll keep you posted." Samantha hung up and sat back in her chair. "Bloody hell Georgie you might have been right all along."

The rest of Samantha's day dragged by. She had called Georgina and left a message without telling her very much, only that she wanted to meet up again as soon as possible. She didn't want to frighten her friend because she had no proof. But her gut feeling was telling her that something was definitely not right, and they both needed to find out for sure.

Samantha had decided to drive to Georgina's without calling her first and enlisted Martin's help from the office. Besides the fact that she knew he worked out regularly at the gym, he took this client on in her absence. So, he didn't need much persuading, especially when she explained her fears to him.

On route, Samantha's phone pinged, and she pulled over and read the message. "Will be home by six. Are you all right?" Typical Georgina, she thought, always thinking of others. "I'm okay and on my way." She kept the text short and sweet and carried on towards Georgina's.

"How are we going to play this, Sam?" Martin asked as they stepped out of the car and walked towards the house. "Good question Martin. The truth is I don't know. But let's not jump straight in and make assumptions."

Once again, the main front door was unlocked and off the latch when Samantha turned the handle and pushed. They both looked at each other. "It was open last time I came as well." She said to Martin, who looked around and indicated with his eyes that she looked up. There were two tiny cameras, one aimed down the path to the gate, the other pointing directly at the door.

"Those aren't your standard CCTV," Martin said quietly. "I agree. Let's get to Georgie's room and work out our next move." Samantha didn't wait for a reply. She was through the door and up the stairs, leaving Martin in her wake.

"Georgina, it's Sam, and I've brought a friend." She knocked and looked back for Martin. "If he ever gets here, that is." Georgina opened the door and greeted her friend with a hug. She then looked around the landing. "I thought you had someone with you?" She queried, looking perplexed.

Samantha sighed. "I did at the front door. Where the hell is he?" She walked to the top of the stairs. "Martin, where are you?"

"Down here. I think you might need to call the police." Samantha didn't hesitate. She knew Martin well enough and took her phone from her back pocket. "What do I tell them?" She yelled down, placing her hand on the banister as her phone rang.

"Tell them I have a seriously nasty little man in my clutches." The girls looked at each other and rushed down the stairs together. At the bottom, Georgina could see Desmond's door was wide open. "In here," Martin shouted, having heard the thundering sound of footsteps pounding on the threadbare carpet.

They nervously walked in together, not knowing what to expect. The sight of Martin crouched over Desmond, with one knee firmly in his back and both hands around his neck and head squashing it into the carpet. Made them both gasp. "Check the bedroom, but don't touch anything," He said, looking up. They both walked tentatively towards the open door and saw the bank of large screens spread across a wooden worktop. Georgina's hand flew up to her mouth when she saw herself stepping out of the shower.

Samantha ushered her away and guided her back towards Martin. "Sorry, you had to see that." Martin looked up at Georgina and automatically pressed harder down on Desmond's head. "I noticed his door was open a crack and that he was spying on us. I did knock before I pushed it open." He made light of the fact before carrying on. "It seems I was a little heavy-handed because he was scrabbling to his feet and trying to close his bedroom door when I walked in. But I got there first. Saw that," Martin nodded to the bedroom. "And, so, here we are."

Samantha hugged Georgina, who sobbed into her shoulder. At least it was all over, and her instincts had been right all along. Downside? Samantha would probably have to find her friend somewhere else to live once he was in his rightful place, behind bars.

ALWAYS CLOSE

Inspired by: STAND BY ME
Performed by BEN E. KING

The raging storm had been relentless all night, and even though it was nearly morning, Nalani knew that she should have taken the advice to evacuate the house. When the Kauai police came before dark, warning the few residents who lived at the bottom of the hillside to move into town, she ignored their pleas. Insisting on staying in her maternal home and seeing out the storm. Even though it had been raining on and off for three days, no one was going to force her to leave.

Now, everything had changed. The power to her single-storey two-bedroomed house had gone, and still, the rain battered away at her home. She feared the roof would be ripped off at any moment with all the crashing and banging going on outside. It was all very frightening. She knew she had made a terrible mistake in staying.

Nalani hadn't moved from beneath the kitchen table in the past hour, and she was now becoming hysterical, screaming every time some solid object hit the building. She tried to calm herself by thinking of her late father and what he would have done in a situation like this.

"He would have left when the police advised him to," Nalani muttered to herself as she shone her torch around the room, trying to see if any rainwater was seeping in. Nothing looked amiss, and she let out a gentle sigh of relief. The wooden front door suddenly flew open and clattered back and forth. The strong wind almost ripped the flimsy inner screen door from its hinges. Leaving it hanging limply at a strange angle.

Nalani scrambled from beneath the table and rushed across the room. The driving rain and winds were doing their utmost to force their way into her home, and she was just as determined to keep them out. Nalani had to use her shoulder plus all her strength to push the door closed once again, and then she quickly wedged the back of a chair beneath the handle as an added precaution.

As she turned to go back to the table's relative safety, she saw a man's bulky figure standing in the semi-darkness. She screamed, pointed her torch straight at him, and quickly realised that her father was standing there. Nalani dashed across the room, her arms open as tears of joy ran down her cheeks.

She stopped just short of the back wall of the house, her hands nearly knocking over several of the many books stacked on the shelves. Nalani turned on her heels and pointed the torch towards the front door. There was no one else there. She was completely alone. The tears of joy changed to ones of anger and sadness. Her father had died less than a year ago. The fishing boat and his body were never found.

Nalani stood silently, staring straight ahead.

She had seen him here in their house. She took a deep breath before she spoke. "What do I do now, old man?" She whispered, reflecting on her choice of words. She had been calling him *old man* since she was sixteen. She was now twenty-one. It had originally been in anger but had quickly changed to a term of endearment.

She had lost her temper with him one morning when he struggled to push his boat off the beach. She had accused him of being too old to fish and that she should take over, allowing him to rest in his hammock and sleep all day. He had laughed at her for calling him old and had chased her along the shoreline, splashing foaming sea water at her as she yelled with delight, skipping and jumping through the incoming waves.

Even with the rampant storm outside, the place was eerily quiet. But she felt safe as if she were somehow cocooned inside a giant spiritual bubble. She sensed the house was different. She wasn't alone anymore. Her father was here, of that she had no doubt. She had seen him standing there, arms folded across his broad chest, in his typical masculine pose. She had so many photos of him standing like that.

"So, old man. You are here, but it seems that the cat has got your tongue. Well, I can live with that. Having you close is comforting in a way. I just need to make a few decisions like, stay or go?" The heavy banging and rattling of the roof, plus the loud creaking and growling, were enough to force her hand. "You or something is telling me to get out of here and now." She shouted above the noise.

Nalani dashed into her parent's bedroom and retrieved her prepacked rucksack and walking boots.

Even though she had been adamant about not leaving, ignoring the female police officer's pleas to come with them, she had the presence of mind to fill her rucksack with fruit, water, and clothing.

She had moved into the larger bedroom on the day her father had been reported missing. Sleeping in his bed had been some comfort as she waited for news. After that, she couldn't bring herself to return to her own room. She always felt he was there with her, which helped her sleep more easily.

Nalani hadn't even reached the front door before some great force hit the back of the house, and the whole building suddenly lurched forward. She was thrown to the floor and propelled towards the little kitchen, off the main room. Then the wooden building leaned and buckled in the other direction, and she immediately changed track, now being flung back towards her bedroom. She crashed into the closed door, which opened on impact, allowing her to roll up against her bed.

Dazed and confused, Nalani staggered to her feet, trying desperately to find something solid to grip. The angle of the moving house now meant that everything in the room was heading towards the front door. Nalani quickly sat and let the momentum move her. It wasn't particularly fast, so she could avoid unsavoury hard objects. That didn't stop some of her books from the shelving behind her from clattering into her back.

Within seconds she was sitting beneath the front window. One pane of glass had already shattered, leaving sharp shards around her. She edged away from the danger and, now sitting by the door, used the chair to help stand up. She quickly realised that she had done an excellent job securing the chair beneath the door handle because it wouldn't budge. A large palm tree came to her rescue.

Out of nowhere, one palm tree came crashing through the window she had just been sitting beneath, and another battered the front door open, ripping it off its hinges and flinging the stubborn chair and door to the back of the house, both missing her by inches. Nalani grabbed at the open framework and clung on as branches, bushes, and small uprooted trees rushed through the gap. The storm was filling her home with debris and rubbish at such an alarming rate that she feared she would soon become trapped.

Outside it was lighter than she thought it would be. The rain had nearly stopped and was nothing more than a drizzle. The sun was out there somewhere, but the storm clouds had complete control, and it was more like dusk than early morning. Nalani gasped when she saw a river of thick mud rushing down the narrow gully less than ten feet away from her. She needed to move fast and safely. Most of the higher ground was behind her, and so she ran around the side of her house. What greeted her made her scream and run back the way she had just come.

A second mudflow was descending the hillside straight at her, moving quicker and much broader than the one in the gully. Out of the corner of her eye, Nalani saw the place where she was born become overtaken, as wood splintered and snapped like tiny matchsticks and became completely engulfed in the tide of brown mud. Now, it was literally just ten feet behind her and getting closer by the second.

Away to her right, a steep rise in the ground might save her if she could get there in time and scramble up it. She was now clawing at the ground, trying desperately to find anything that would support her weight, allowing her to move further away from the river of death. Her fingers wrapped around the vast tangled roots of an Ironwood tree, and she levered herself up past the standing trunk and then kept running up the higher ground from one tree to another.

At last, she felt safe. Down below, her home and everything she owned had disappeared. There was nothing but a small section of roof to see as the two mudslides now joined forces and swallowed everything in their wake. Nalani couldn't control her emotions, and salty tears flowed freely down her face. She wiped them away to the best of her ability using the back of her hand. Nalani knew the Hawaiian Island very well. She had never lived anywhere else, but now she was feeling disorientated, lost even, just yards from her home.

"So, which way, old man?" She asked, sniffing deeply. The wind further up the hillside whistled gently through the trees ahead of her. "Okay, left it is." She replied back as if she had received positive, clear instructions. Nalani pushed on, the day getting brighter as the sun broke through the menacing clouds and the rain finally ceased.

As she trudged up the steep wooded hillside, she thought more and more of her father. How he had helped her cope when her mother had died suddenly, and how he gently prepared her for his own inevitable death. Even though he was stolen from her life much too early, he was a philosopher reading the stars and the elements. The cloud formation told him certain things would happen, and they always did.

"Where there is wind, there is life." She reminded herself it was one of his favourite sayings, and she had heard it almost daily. She missed him so much, and now everything had gone, all the family photos, the weird stuff he would find floating in the sea and then place on the front porch. They all had a story to tell, and his imagination was endless.

Before long, Nalani was clear of the forest and scrambling up through wet lush green vegetation, going higher and higher up the steep hillside. Every weary step she hoped was taking her further away from danger but also civilisation. There were no houses up here, just the occasional hiking trail guiding brave tourist adventurers deeper and deeper into the unknown.

Nalani stood staring up ahead. The powerful storm had blown over several small pine trees, and she appeared to be standing on a narrow ridge with a sheer drop on either side. Her way seemed blocked, and the thought of turning back crossed her mind until she saw a palm tree further up the ridge directly in front of her.

It looked so odd. The few trees around here were young Cook pines, and this palm tree was uncharacteristically out of place. Nalani was drawn to it like a magnet, and she couldn't stop looking at it. The moving palm leaves hypnotised her, they were swaying in all directions, and she took it as a sign.

The single track led straight along the tight ridge towards the palm tree, making her think that perhaps walkers were drawn to it as she was. She climbed over the first two pine trees easily, but now a couple were lying across each other. She began scrambling over the scaly, rough texture of the trunk when the paper-thin strip of bark she was holding onto came away in her hand.

Suddenly she was rolling backward and tumbling head over heels off the trail and over the ridge edge. Nalani tried desperately to grab at anything as she rolled further down into the valley. The long thin blades of wet grass ripped through her fingers as she tried to cling on and stop her speeding descent into the unknown.

Her journey ended abruptly and painfully when she crashed into a large broken tree branch. She felt the sharp stinging pain in her side before she realised she had stopped falling. Though she was dazed, her hand automatically went straight to the point of pain as she attempted to sit up. There was blood on her fingers, which seemed to make the pain in her side feel worse.

Nalani was pleased that her rucksack was still attached to her back, even though, on inspection, she saw that the top flap had been ripped open. She quickly ascertained that she hadn't lost anything in her fall and opened a bottle of water. She first quenched her dry throat before pouring the rest of the water over the wound.

She couldn't see how nasty the wound was, but she knew it was bleeding profusely. Taking off her windcheater and then her blouse, she ripped it as best she could and then wrapped it around her body. Knotting the sleeves together tightly at the front made her wince with pain, but she knew it had to be done.

As she sat precariously on the steep slope, Nalani knew there was a danger of her tumbling further down. She pressed her feet against the thick branch that had caused her injury and gathered her thoughts. The way down was treacherous. It was almost vertical, and she couldn't see the valley floor because of the mist now slowly rising up the hillside. The day was getting warmer, even though she felt shivery and cold, and her teeth were chattering.

She had just started to drink her second bottle of water when she heard the noise for the first time. She sat perfectly still, straining her ears and with her eyes closed as she concentrated. It didn't take her long to confirm her initial thoughts. It was running water. Down in the valley, there was a river, a stream at least, and even she knew what that meant. Follow the source and reach the sea.

Nalani went to stand, but the pain in her side prevented her from doing so. She gripped at her makeshift bandage and adjusted the knot. Taking a deep breath, she slowly shuffled her way through the tall grass. Her legs bent up, one hand on the floor and the other on her wound. It was a slow and challenging journey. She often stopped to check the terrain directly in her path. More than once, she felt giddy and thought she might pass out. Each time she stopped and waited.

Then she saw a trail off to her left. It looked wet and muddy, but at least it wasn't going straight down. It was taking a gentle meandering route. She eased her way over to the nearest point and saw, to her dismay, that there was a ten-foot drop that she would have to negotiate. Nalani had no choice, and she wriggled across on her bottom and let herself fall off the edge and onto the path.

She screamed as the hard thud from the

landing rippled through her body. Her head went backwards and thumped into the mud. Her rucksack helped take some of the force, but she lay there crying as every part of her body hurt. Nalani eventually sat up and checked her wound. The jarring had caused more bleeding, and her whole hand was covered with blood. She needed to carry regardless.

The mud was helping her, and she was moving faster on the trail than she could ever imagine. In some places, the downhill slope was steep enough to let her just sit there and slide slowly without any movement on her part. She went around curve after curve, manoeuvring some with care, but most of the time, she just went with the natural flow and was watchful of what lay ahead.

Suddenly without warning, the whole area opened up. There was a river, but it was a waterfall that she had heard back on the hillside. It roared as it plunged twenty feet from between huge rocks and splashed into the waiting pool below. Nalani struggled to her hands and knees and crawled to the water's edge.

She couldn't even remember which waterfall this was. She wasn't even sure that she had ever been here before, but none of that mattered. This place was for tourists. There were picnic benches dotted everywhere. It was a beautiful sight to behold. It made her smile and helped her forget her aches and pains for a while, at least.

Nalani sat quietly and contemplated her fate. She had at least one more bottle of water, dragon fruit, and bananas in her rucksack. She was utterly exhausted and knew she wouldn't be able to move any time soon. But she also needed medical help.

Although, the wound on her side didn't seem as bad since she had been here resting.

After a few minutes, tiredness began to take over. Nalani felt her eyelids droop, and sleep came within seconds. She dreamt of her father. He was standing at the top of the falls telling her to be strong, that help would soon come. *"Believe in yourself, Nalani. You are strong, and I am always here. You will be safe soon."*

"Miss. Miss, wake up." Nalani opened her eyes, startled and confused, as she felt someone gently rocking her shoulder. "It's okay. I'm Airborne Aviation. I'm here to help you." Nalani managed a smile as everything kicked in. She heard something thrumming above her head and looked up to see the red helicopter hovering over the waterfall.

"Let's get you out of here, Miss." Nalani stood and waited while he attached the safety harness to her. "Hold on, here we go." As he spoke, he waved up at the pilot, and within seconds they were both winched on board.

"You were fortunate. We were looking for a couple of hikers who had set off for the falls two days ago. We had already flown over here once and found nothing, and then the pilot thought he spotted a man waving from the rocks over there." Her rescuer said, pointing down to the top of the waterfall just before the pilot swung the helicopter away. "But there was no one to be seen until I saw you huddled down there. Yes, you were very lucky young lady."

Nalani smiled to herself before she thanked them both profusely for saving her life.

IN THE GROOVE

Inspired by: THE PIANO MAN.
Performed by BILLY JOEL

I've been here in Los Angeles now for just over two years. I left my native England, family, and friends behind with grand ideas. No job waiting for me and very little money in my back pocket. Not only that, but I'm thirty-five this coming August. The clock, as they say, is ticking, and time is running out for me. If my life doesn't start to change soon, I'm not convinced it ever will.

I've always seen myself as the next Tom Cruise or even a budding Bruce Willis. So, I moved here to L. A. with the expectation of making the big time in the movie world. It can't be that difficult. Wrong, there's a problem, a big problem. My face just doesn't seem to fit. I blindly assumed they would love my quaint, quirky English accent, but I've had nothing, no joy, from any of the film companies. I've read and reread my CV. I tweaked it a little here and lied a little bit more there.

I have had a few auditions. I can't remember exactly how many. I found most of them rather depressing, to be honest. Sitting around in a room full of other hopefuls, smiling nervously every time the young lady came out of the office and called out someone's name, wishing it was yours. Only once did I ever manage to get past the first casting. But it wasn't the big time that I was hoping for. It was simply a non-speaking walk-on part.

They wanted an outdoor crowd scene, with twenty people walking down a street in opposite directions, with no other action, just walking and looking straight ahead. The producer had even employed a man with a dog, who they made more fuss of than the actors. What's more, it was a bloody great big black St Bernard of a dog, who followed behind me, sniffing my rear end as if he fancied me.

Just act natural it won't bite, they said. I did my best but still didn't get the job. It seemed that the director didn't like me waving at the camera and grinning like a Cheshire cat. I did my own thing once by stopping suddenly and letting the dog walk past me. I thought it was a good idea, and at least my mom would notice me and perhaps ignore the leading man, who was just a stand-in at the moment. I could have done that, stood by the posh red car, kissed the leading lady, and then opened the car door and watched her slide those extra-long curvy legs into place.

Maybe, my ex-girlfriend was right. Perhaps Jonathan Bloxham-Bloodworth doesn't have a perfect ring to it? Or possibly I do need some dental work done on my teeth. But I actually like the way I can curl my tongue up through the double gap at the front. I've even been asked to do it at the occasional parties that I have attended. Everyone laughed, they were usually drunk, but they did laugh.

So, here I am, working another Saturday night in this supposedly upmarket bar. Wishing I could find an easy way out. Thank God William, the piano player likes me. Well, I guess plying him with drinks helps. He has to talk to me, doesn't he? He has to ask for another beer. I've got his number, though. It's usually every third song, although sometimes he manages to get through four before he indicates that his throat is getting a bit dry, but not very often.

When I first started here, I thought this bartender job would tide me over before I made the big time and became famous. Joe, the owner, always smiled when I told him I might be leaving at the end of the week. I guess he knew me better than I knew myself. He always said the same thing. "Don't be late tomorrow, Johnny boy. You know how much we rely on you."

The bar has changed so much in the last few months since Joe left. When he was here running the place, we used to have a lovely little trio playing nightly, nothing fancy. Single snare drum, guitar, and double bass. They played so nicely and quietly in the background that the customers hardly knew they were there. Then, one day, everything changed, and a piano suddenly arrived without warning. I was the only one in the place at the time. I was there stocking up the bar and rearranging the tables and chairs. Of course, I protested. Joe had said nothing the night before. He had seemed rather glum and moody but not a word of warning.

One of the four burly bruisers stuffed a piece of paper beneath my nose when I challenged him. Then they pushed and shoved the piano until it was finally in place. It took up all the area that the trio did and was almost hanging over the edge of the tiny platform of a stage.

Joe didn't turn up that morning. The truth is, we haven't seen him since. On the busy street, sign writers changed the bar's name from Joe's Place to The Piano Room, and the drink prices went up by half a dollar or so. From that night, we got ourselves a new owner, an extra barmaid called Mandy, and the music changed because we had William on the ivories.

Give credit where credit is due, he did he know how to belt them out? He could change the slowest song into pure unadulterated honky tonk. His fingers were mesmerising when he was going full tilt. To be fair, he had quite a good voice as well.

So, basically, everything changed overnight. The pool table went the next day, as did the card school, the four guys who always sat in the far corner playing poker just upped and left as soon as they saw the changes. Most importantly, the clientele changed, the guys pushing drugs moved out, and the business people moved in. It was like a hurricane had struck. In less than forty-eight hours, the whole place had changed, and William sat at the piano as the kingpin. He was holding court and running the show.

He did requests but always put his own slant on the song. Of course, the words were the same, but the melody and rhythm were altered to suit his style. He was good, he was very good, and in no time at all, he helped fill this place to the rafters. Every night we were stacked out, people coming in to try and forget their troubles, their crap day at the office. The over-demanding manager who pushed and bullied his way through the day. They wanted to leave him far behind, to be a distant memory until tomorrow.

Today was a typical Saturday, and it was well after eight in the evening. William has been here since about five, trying out different numbers. I said earlier that he would do requests, but we have a few plants in the bar, and I don't mean the greenery type. Several of our regulars are given a free beer to shout out certain songs that William is keen to belt out. Having practiced them over a period of time, he usually gives me the nod when he wants one of the stooges to shout up.

Mandy, the barmaid, isn't the brightest bulb on the circuit. She still hasn't worked it out. The look of amazement on her young face when she hears someone call out Strangers in the Night, and William goes straight into the opening bars before starting the first chorus. Mandy has so much to learn, especially as she's reading politics in her spare time and tells anyone who will listen that it won't be long before she runs for Congress. I suppose she's a little like me, really, working here all the hours that God made, living on dreams, believing that a better life is just around the corner.

Even on a Saturday, some of the customers are the same, not all business people, although there are a few who do nip out for the quick martini or gin and tonic. Saturdays are usually reserved for the husband's escaping for a couple of hours while the wife tucks the kids up in bed and reads them a story.

Stefan, the boss, is in tonight. He stays a little longer at the weekends. Usually, during the week, he won't last long, he just likes to flip in, check that the place is doing okay, and then he's off for the rest of the night. Though, he always comes back just before we close. He always insists on removing the takings. I can understand that, as there can't be many places in L.A. that aren't susceptible to being broken into at night.

He likes to walk around the tables slapping people on the back, asking how they are as if he's known them forever when he is absolutely crap at remembering names. Most just nod and say very little. Occasionally, one will respond, and Stefan will then have to stand there smiling sweetly, listening to the customer, and it's always the one with the morbid life story. The person with nothing going for him. Single, divorced, some married, but wishing they were divorced.

He never seems to grasp that not everyone's life is as straightforward as his appears to be. Stephan's life is already mapped out, with his plans laid bare before him. He has everything that he wants and more. Most customers coming here to The Piano Room are lost souls moving through their own little worlds. Surviving from one day to another, their eyes glazed over, moving zombies dying of boredom. I've seen them so often, spoken with them, poured some of them their last drink. Stephan sees none of that. He is too embroiled in his own world of money and power.

William is in excellent form tonight, and he has their full attention. It's as though they are hanging on his every word and that every song is just for them and no one else. He tells them about finding love and then losing it to someone else. A man at the bar, standing next to me, raises his beer glass as a solemn salute that he understands. William spots his actions and points a finger in his direction before repeating the verse just for him.

"Yea," the man happily yells back and raises

his glass even higher. They both smile at each other. William has this particular kind of rapport with some customers. Perhaps he's been there himself. Hurt, broken by love. He had his dreams shattered by some woman to whom he gave his heart and body, only for her to toy with his emotions before casting him aside.

My mistake. I got carried away there for a minute. I guess I was reminiscing more about how my ex, Lucy, treated me. The fact is, I know nothing about William or his private life, but he's heard my tale of woe so often that he could probably write a song about it. The times that I've told him about how Lucy didn't believe in me. How she wouldn't leave England and move to Los Angeles to be with me. Her friends were more important to her than I was. She didn't want to help me chase my dream of becoming a movie star.

Most nights since he's been here, William has done alright. The punters seem to get a real kick out of dropping money into his tips jar. It's an old-fashioned glass-shaped biscuit barrel with the word "Cookies" embossed several times around the neck. It stands on top of the piano, meaning they must try to drop whatever they feel is appropriate. But they do this willingly.

Some walk over slowly, rhythmically rattling the loose change from a round of drinks in their cupped hands. They want to be seen, it's their way of saying thank you to him, and they want everyone in the room to know what they are doing. Money is scarce in these awful times.

The shyer ones often get me to do their dirty work for them. "Stick it in Will's cookie jar." That said, I have often been given a five-dollar bill and even the occasional ten dollars. I always fold them neatly and let William know who the tipper is, especially if I know the customer's name, because I know William will call him out and thank him. Often dedicating the next song to him.

Here we go. It's that time of night already. Stephan, the boss, is doing his rounds, sauntering between the tables, smiling sweetly, and nodding his head when he hears that a customer is happy. He will walk over to the piano in a minute. He always does. Stephan revels in it, standing there clapping and pointing at William when he finishes a number. He's so embarrassing to watch. As if anyone in the room really believes he cares.

From there, he will wander over to the bar and spoil the pretence by asking me how many drinks William has had. I lie. I always lie. William and his piano playing bring the punters in, not anything else. Not me or Mandy, and certainly not Stephan's charm. No, they want their little bit of escapism, their freedom from work and everyday stress, if only for a song or two.

He provides that. He is the man that they believe in, be it just for tonight only. In a way, he is their saviour. Perhaps even, in some cases, their very last hope. They may not realise that as they sit here listening to him playing, joining in, humming, or singing along quietly, but it's true. William is helping to keep some of them alive, helping them to forget tomorrow's troubles.

Life out there in the big city is ugly, and nothing is back to normal. World recession is just around the corner, and in some parts of America, it has already arrived and is on full throttle. We are being driven to disaster. It's the 1929 Wall Street crash all over again, and we do not know the answer. No one does. But he is doing his little bit, helping to keep some of them alive. Some of them might not be here this time tomorrow without William, the piano man.

REJECTED LOVE

Inspired by: SYLVIA'S MOTHER.
Performed by DOCTOR HOOK

Nothing was going to bring her back. He knew that one hundred percent. Heaven knows he had tried everything humanly possible, flowers, cards, messages of devotion. He had even declared his undying love for her on his Facebook page, accepting the stick and sarcastic comments from his so-called friends in the process.

John Anderson didn't know which way to turn next. He was so in love with this woman that she was in his head twenty-four-seven. He just couldn't stop thinking about her. Everything around him was crumbling. Even his job was now in jeopardy. He was losing the plot, and all because of this woman. He had already taken two weeks of annual leave and, to make matters worse, he was now calling in sick. He wasn't sleeping at night. All he was managing to do was mope about the house all day.

John's life was a mess until divine intervention stepped in the way it so often seemed to do. He forced himself to make an effort to get out of the house. During a chance meeting in a bar with an old friend, he discovered, after a few beers, that the love of his life was getting married. Not only that, but his friend knew the date, time, and place. That meeting changed his life. He suddenly had a new purpose about him. He was making plans, getting himself together.

Friday morning and John Anderson had only twenty-four hours to travel the one thousand five hundred miles to find her. What he was going to do then, the truth was, he still had no idea. He just knew he couldn't sit at home and do nothing because he would regret that for the rest of his life.

He messaged his boss. "Family crisis, need seventy-two hours." That was all he said before purposely leaving his phone at home and heading out of the door. As the New York taxi headed for John F. Kennedy airport, he began to realise that being so blunt to his employer may not have been a good idea. But he was a man possessed and on a mission that involved the woman he loved. He didn't have time for complicated explanations. She was getting married tomorrow, and he needed to be there.

Sitting around JFK gave him time to think. He was hatching a plan. The trouble with that was one-sided love is blinkered and seldom worked. But that wasn't going to stop him from trying. Nothing was. He was so engrossed in thought and staring into his coffee cup that he hadn't heard his name called as the final passenger to board until it was almost too late.

Houston, Texas, didn't seem very appealing as he stared out of the plane's tiny window. He wasn't impressed by the tall buildings. They looked like little pieces of Lego compared to the New York skyscrapers. The landing was bumpy, it seemed to take forever to disembark, and every taxi was taken once outside of the terminal in the blazing afternoon sun. He was already beginning to feel the pressure of attempting the impossible.

Time-wise, though, he was ahead of himself. Everything had panned out better than he could ever have imagined. There had been a plane leaving New York that morning, and with flight time and sitting around time, it was just after four in the afternoon when his taxi pulled up outside the front of a Holiday Inn. If they had a room, which the taxi driver had more or less guaranteed, he would start to feel a little happier.

He sat alone. He had eaten and was sipping at his cold beer. His head was a jumble of thoughts. He had travelled all this way, intending to stop the woman he loved from getting married. How was that going to work? Could he really stop her from marrying the man she loved?

Perhaps he could. His old friend back in New York admitted that she had only just met this man, who had seemingly swept her off her feet. John had even suggested that maybe she was on the rebound from him and that she wasn't thinking straight. Ray had shaken his head and explained that he had met this knight in shining armour. He had seen their love for each other, and it seemed to be the real deal.

John Anderson was so deep in his own misery, that it took him a while to notice the young lady now standing at the edge of his table. It wasn't until he had the weird feeling of being watched that he looked up and saw her. She smiled cheerfully and waited. When there was no response, she spoke to him. "Hi, I couldn't help but notice that you seemed a little downcast. May I sit?" John shrugged and nodded at the empty chair. This wasn't what he needed right now. Another beer would have been nearer the mark.

"So, I guess I'm right." He looked straight at her and waited. "And it's probably a woman? It usually is. Hangdog eyes staring into a glass of beer, a meal half eaten." It was now her turn to shrug before she introduced herself properly, stretching her hand across the table. "Sandie Jordan, Philosopher, agony aunt, and a little bit tipsy." Her cheery smile was back, and he couldn't help but smile as he checked his watch. It was only after six o'clock, and this woman admitted to being under the influence of alcohol.

"John Anderson, pleased to meet you, Sandie." Her long slender fingers were soft and warm to his touch. "You're right, of course, about the woman." He released her hand and noticed how she gently caressed it with the other one as if she were feeling the vibes. "Would you like a drink?" He asked, calling the waitress over at the same time.

"No, thank you, John Anderson. As I said, I'm a little tipsy now, and another one would probably send me over the edge." He stopped the waitress from coming any closer. "And, would that be a bad thing?"

"Oh yes, I think it would. I would probably tell you all the wrong things to do. Give you all the wrong signals, and make your situation even worse than it is now."

"Well, that's very honest of you, Sandie Jordan. I think I will appreciate that in the morning. You certainly are a philosopher." They both laughed. "And now I suppose I'm going to get the full agony aunt bit?"

"If you want it, yes. It's free and impartial, and I'm a good listener. So, go for it." Sandie sat back and waited.

"Once upon a time." He began, and they both started laughing so loudly that they turned around, embarrassed to see if anyone was looking at them. It just made them laugh even more when they realised they were the only two in the restaurant area.

"Shall we go and sit in the lobby? I'm sure it's a lot more comfortable there?" Sandie nodded, and they walked arm-in-arm. The desk clerk smiled as they strolled past him, and he watched them until they stopped by two sizeable brown leather Chesterfield sofas close enough to have one each and talk. He was there at their side in seconds. "Would two coffees be in order?" He asked, keeping his single-minded thoughts to himself.

"Black for me, please," Sandie replied.

"Make that two, then, please," John added before looking back to Sandie. "Now, where was I?" he asked, smiling.

"Well, you can skip the intro." Sandie laughed back at him.

"Point taken. Okay, I've just flown halfway across the country to try and stop the woman I love from marrying someone else." Sandie pursed her lips together and nodded approvingly.

"Wow, I'm impressed." She sat back and crossed her long slender legs. He watched her face. She was deep in thought, her blue eyes staring straight ahead, focused on nothing important. The stillness between them hung like an invisible veil. It wasn't an awkward silence, far from it. To both of them, it felt comfortable as they sat reflecting on the enormity of the task.

Sandie had spoken to him, but he hadn't heard her. "Sorry!" He put his hand up. "What did you say?" She waited as their coffees arrived. They both nodded their thanks.

"Have you really thought this through?" She began. "My head is telling me that if she is marrying someone else, it's because she wants to." John frowned at her words. It wasn't what he wanted to hear. He was telling her his deepest secrets. He wanted encouragement from her, not something he had already worked out for himself. Stating the obvious was of no help to him.

"I have thought about nothing else. But sitting at home and not confronting the problem was killing me. I have to ask the question."

"Even though you know the answer?"

"Yes. Yes. I need to ask the question. Okay!" His anger rose, and he knew he was out of line. "Sorry, it's just…." He couldn't finish his sentence. Sandie leaned forward and picked up her cup and saucer. "You need to know for sure. I get it. But if you love this woman as much as you say you do. Are you really going to spoil her special moment?"

Without hesitation, John nodded his head and mouthed, "Yes." Sandie pulled a face of disapproval. He felt a pang of disappointment, and he thought she would listen, not condemn every word he said. She saw the look he was giving her and knew it was now her turn to apologise. "Sorry. I need to hear the whole story before passing judgment."

"You make it sound as if I'm on trial?" He retorted.

"Well, in a way, you are. She is making a life-changing decision, and you are considering the possibility of wrecking it, perhaps to satisfy your ego. So, yes John, I do believe that you are on trial."

Sandie sipped her coffee and looked him full in the eyes. He used her drinking to take on board some liquid of his own. They both sat quietly, staring at each other.

"Look, Sandie. I know you offered to help, but I think you will automatically come down on her side of the fence. You see me as the aggressive one, someone wanting revenge. If I can't have her, then no one can. That kind of thing."

"Well, you said it first. So, it must have been in your subconscious. Even if you never admit that out loud, it was there, just waiting for the right moment to surface." John sat back and blew his cheeks out. "Wow, hold on a minute, you're talking way out of my league here. I didn't think that at all." Sandie placed her coffee down, raised her arms, and smiled at him.

"Isn't that precisely what I just said?" They were both shaking their heads at each other. Neither person was willing to admit defeat. Sandie knew this would end as a stalemate, so she decided to try and conclude the conversation. "Last word on the matter because we are never going to agree. You know that the woman you love is going to get married tomorrow. You also know that she doesn't love you. No matter how much that hurts. That's the truth here, John. I'm sorry, but she doesn't love you."

She watched as his head dropped to his chest and waited for him to compose himself before continuing. "That, I'm afraid, is the bottom line. Your love is all one way, and whatever you think you can do about it, I doubt that that is true. So, let it go, John. Stop chasing after something that you can't have. Leave the woman you love in peace, and move on."

John Anderson sat at the back of the church. He had positioned himself as far away from the centre aisle that led down to the altar as possible. He acted the part very well, looking inconspicuous, wearing a dark suit and a plain silk blue tie.

He watched the constant stream of family and wedding guests filing into the church, taking their places as they shuffled between the wooden pews. Seeing everyone arrive started the adrenaline pumping through his body. Suddenly, he was beginning to feel all sorts of different emotions. Jealousy and envy were there, churning away at his innards, eating into his feelings, and leaving a nasty acid taste in his mouth.

He saw the two young men enter the church and knew immediately from the smiles and nods that the groom and best man had arrived. The way some of the guests near the centre aisle singled out one of them, speaking quietly with him and shaking his hand. He quickly learned who the intended was, and the infectious smile on his face was also a giveaway.

People chatted quietly, and someone next to him asked if he was with the bride or groom. He felt obliged to answer and muttered the bride. The woman turned the other way and spoke with the man she had arrived with. John managed a smile to himself. She was probably saying that he looked miserable. Which, of course, he was. Unless he did something, he was about to witness the loss of the woman he loved.

The bridal march struck up, and the church fell silent. People began to turn their heads and watch, smiling as the bride, dressed in her full-length white wedding dress, slowly walked down the aisle towards her future husband. The first thing John noticed was her beaming smile. She looked happy and radiant. He turned his head away quickly as she glanced over in his direction.

He suddenly felt remorse as he slowly turned back, daring to check if she had seen him and was now staring at him. He had seen that look in her eyes. The bottom line was he had seen it in both of their eyes, and although it made him envious, it also made him realise that he was wrong. The love of his life wasn't the love of his life anymore. She was now someone else's.

John Anderson knew he shouldn't still be sitting there listening to the service. That he should have walked out of the church some time ago, but something was making him stay. Whenever he convinced himself to leave, something inside told him to stay. His head and eyes wanted to witness the event, but his heart wanted him to get out while he could. Very shortly, it was all going to become very painful.

Then it happened as if from nowhere, the vicar asked the question he dreaded hearing. He closed his eyes, and his throat suddenly went dry and constricted. He tried hard to swallow, but it was almost impossible. He rose to his feet, gripping the back of the wooden pew to steady himself. "Leave. Get out now." The voice in his head was loud and clear.

He turned and walked quickly across the flagstones of the church, his footsteps loud and echoing. He stopped at the centre aisle and stood straight and tall.

"Yes, I do. I have something to say." He shouted down the church towards the vicar. His heart started racing as he saw everyone turn to face him. The bride and groom were the last to react. He saw the look of horror on her face. Her hand went towards her mouth, and she looked across at the man standing at her side. She knew he had no idea what was going on.

John Anderson took a deep breath. "I just wanted to say. "I love you, and farewell. Perhaps in another lifetime, maybe!" He shrugged at the thought. "Adios, sayonara and be happy." Without hesitating, he turned and walked out of the church.

As he walked down the old stone steps and into the Houston sunshine, his eyes were full of salty tears, but he had done something. It wasn't as he had planned, but he had broken the link and cut the final tie between them. Sandie had been right, and he needed to move on. Take things slowly, to wait until his heart is fully repaired and healed. Then he might love again.

He waved and managed a smile. There was Sandie, as promised, waiting for him. If anyone had the power to mend a broken heart, he felt sure that she did. At least it was worth a try.

MAKING DO

Inspired by: PAPER RINGS.
Performed by TAYLOR SWIFT

War-torn Ukraine offered them nothing on their special day, but they were in love and, as we know, that particular emotion knows no boundaries. It doesn't stop existing just because the church you were about to get married in is now in ruins. Virtually flattened to the ground by yesterday's heavy shelling. Love is bigger than that, much, much bigger.

Yeva was ready and dressed. She looked lovely in her mother's full-length white wedding gown. She wore a simple crown of pink and white peonies, complete with a small bouquet of matching flowers, that lay momentarily undisturbed on the kitchen table. She was ready, and nothing was going to stop her from marrying the man she loved.

"It will be fine, Momma. Feliks has sent word. He and his friends spent most of the night clearing splintered wood and heaving rubble away. The church may not have a roof, but the altar is ready, and so is the priest." Yeva hugged her worried mother before looking into her eyes. "We will get married this afternoon. Nothing is going to stop us." Her mother smiled at her daughter's words, proud of her determination but worried nonetheless.

In the last twenty-four hours, so much had changed. Yeva was now going to have to walk to the church. The road had been completely obliterated, and in its place were two huge deep craters and crumbled buildings. No vehicles could get through that mess.

In their determination to marry, Yeva and Feliks abandoned the traditional ritual of the couple visiting both sets of parents in a combined ceremony. Feliks had also been to his future wife's house twice, and he had even seen her in her wedding dress that morning, but none of that mattered. Even when his future mother-in-law tried to forbid him from stepping into the house, the young couple were having none of it.

"Momma, it's okay. Feliks and I need to talk. Everything is different now. Trust me. We know what we're doing." Once again, Yeva's mother backed down, and again her heart was filled with dread and worry. She didn't need someone to tell her that the Russians were closing in. She knew that. Perhaps they were already here, hiding in the woods, waiting for orders to advance, and shoot at anything or anybody that moved.

Yeva checked her phone, and it was time to go. She took a deep breath and ushered her younger sister Galyna to her side before stepping out of the house. She smiled at her mother, who was waiting nervously in the late June sunshine. She was clutching her bag and a small posy of flowers, which she handed to Galyna, who was in attendance as a bridesmaid.

The walk to the crumbled church would take them about twenty minutes and right through the heart of the village. Neighbours stepped out onto the road and applauded as the trio passed. Some of the older ones went back indoors, while the rest formed a line and walked behind. Friends of the family, couples who had once married at the church, mothers with small children. They were all coming to the wedding.

As they walked through the town, women placed their sparse shopping bags down and did the same, clapping and shouting words of encouragement. Yeva acknowledged them with a wave and a smile. Again people joined the procession. They wanted to show their solidarity. Everyone knew the importance of not giving in under these extreme circumstances. Life would go on, no matter what the Russians thought.

As they walked along the edge of the two large craters, Yeva couldn't stop herself from looking down and seeing the destruction of war up close. Her younger sister fumbled to find her hand. As their fingers locked together, Yeva looked across at her and smiled before squeezing gently. She tried to put on a brave face, but her head was filled with horrific images.

Now, she couldn't help but think of her father. She wished he could see her now, strong, brave, and determined. He was officially classed as missing in action. He had been with a group of seven other soldiers when the missile struck the building they were hiding in. Only one returned to tell the tale; unfortunately for Yeva and her family, it wasn't the right one. But she still believed that he was alive, a prisoner of war, maybe. Or he was lying wounded in some remote hospital.

They were on the final approach, and the

church was just over the brow of the hill. By now, they would normally be able to see the dome with its cross, but that was all gone. The skyline was empty, except for the rolling clouds far in the distance. It saddened Yeva but made her all the more determined that the wedding should go on.

Yeva couldn't believe her eyes as the church finally came into view. Where originally, two rows of birch trees had formed an avenue on either side of the path, there were now alternating large blue and yellow oil drums lining the route. She couldn't help but touch one as they passed. Now she knew what Feliks had meant when he said they had spent some of the night clearing splintered wood away.

Behind the three women, relatives, friends, guests, and the unknown applauded when they reached and saw the oil drums for the first time. Yeva couldn't control the smile on her face, and it was getting bigger and bigger by the second. People were now rhythmically beating their hands on the oil drum tops. It wasn't the most fantastic sound in the world, but it seemed that her wedding day was turning into a carnival. That made her very happy.

Up ahead, Yeva could see Feliks, the man she was about to marry. He seemed to stand firm and tall, looking very smart in his dark suit, flanked by his two eldest brothers. All three were facing the altar. Off to the right, the younger brothers of the groom's family were standing with their parents, both looking back, trying to see the bride.

As the procession got closer to the church, Yeva realised, to her horror, how little there was of the building standing. Two walls were gone, blown away by the explosion. The area behind the altar where Feliks and his brothers were standing was bare. The beautiful wooden icons were missing. There should have been four large panels hanging on either side of a big gold-coloured cross.

Before this terrible war, people had travelled to see them, and now they were gone. The cross was still there, it had snapped in two places, but someone had propped it up at a jaunty angle as a sign of resistance. Yeva nodded her approval everyone seemed determined that their wedding would happen.

They were starting their married life together with nothing. There was no space with Feliks and his large family, so they had no choice but to move in with her mother and sister. Life would still be cramped in the little two-bedroomed house, but it would have been almost impossible if Galyna hadn't agreed to move into her mother's bed and allow Feliks to sleep in hers.

None of that mattered. They would be together, and that was all they cared about. They would manage and take on whatever life threw at them. Even this stupid, senseless war wasn't powerful enough to halt true love in its tracks. Nothing could. Yeva believed that with all her heart and soul.

The priest held a small velvet cushion in both hands and invited Feliks to place their wedding rings on it. Feliks looked up from the red cushion, shrugged, and shook his head. "We have nothing. This suit is not mine. This shirt belongs to a neighbour, and this." He touched the neck of the white shirt. "Is a piece of silk my mother found and fashioned into a tie for me. We are in love, and we want to be married. That is all." Feliks bowed his head as he fought back the tears.

Yeva's mother automatically began pulling frantically at her own wedding band. She tugged and tugged desperately, trying to remove it, but her fingers were thicker now than when she first married, and the ring didn't want to move. She stopped and smiled weakly as her younger daughter gently patted her back.

Behind Yeva's mother, a woman quickly removed her ring, tapped her on the shoulder, and, as she turned, pressed it into the palm of her hand, giving her a reassuring smile at the same time.

She nodded as Yeva's mother looked at the broad gold band. "Take it. Please." Yeva's mother stretched over and hugged the woman whose name she didn't know before walking forward and passing it to the priest, who smiled and mouthed a *thank you* to her.

Feliks and Yeva turned around as they heard the commotion behind them. Men and women, some complete strangers, others recognised faces from around the town, were now stepping towards the altar, removing their symbolic wedding rings and placing them on the cushion.

"It seems you do have rings, after all." The priest said, smiling. Yeva and Feliks turned to the congregation and applauded. There were no words powerful enough to say how they felt at this moment in time.

The couple looked at each other and smiled. They had both chosen a ring. The lady who gave hers to Yeva's mother had fitted perfectly, and Yeva waved to her as a thank you. Feliks found a ring on his second attempt, and the priest had already offered the others for collection.

Everyone there heard the distinctive rumbling of the tank before they saw it. Heads were turning in all directions. Eventually, someone pointed across the valley towards the wide track that split the pine forest in half. The tank had by now cleared the trees and was making its way through a field of sunflowers. Behind it followed three more tanks also cutting a swath, all clearly showing a large white Z on their armoured turrets.

People attending the wedding gasped and began mumbling among themselves. They were frightened, panic written on their faces as the chatter became louder. Some people left, hurrying back down the hill to be with their loved ones, hoping to arrive home before the tanks entered the village. Others stood staring in disbelief, their hands covering their mouths.

The priest raised his arms. "Stay calm, everyone. Please just stay calm." His words fell on deaf ears. Children behind the church who had been playing what they called Cat and Mice, where one chased the other until caught, were now being rounded up by anxious mothers and brought under their control.

Yeva and Feliks felt their hearts sink. It seemed that their special day was about to be ruined. They looked to the priest for support. He frowned and shook his head.

"I'm sorry I cannot carry on with the service. I need to get people to safety." He gestured with his hands as if it were out of his control.

"We are here. Please just do it now, quickly, if you like. As long as we are officially married, we don't care." Feliks was begging, his hands together as if in prayer. The priest moved away from the couple and watched the armoured vehicles as they trundled through the following field, leaving four broad lines of flattened crops in their wake.

"They are not turning this way." He said excitedly. "Look, everyone, they are going around the far side of the village." The young couple rushed over to where he was standing. Those that still remained joined them. Some began cheering, dancing up and down, and clapping with delight.

Then as if on cue, the last tank suddenly veered to the right and headed in their direction. It ploughed through a white picket fence that had once been a land boundary to someone's property and proceeded to crush and push a car in its path to one side. Some groaned their disappointment, and the more frightened ones watching fled.

The remaining villagers watched silently as the tank slowly chugged up the hill along the path leading to the church. The priest knew there was little time left. "Quickly this way." He shouted as he hurried to the south wall, which was still partially standing. Yeva checked that her mother and sister were nearby and ready to move. Feliks also ushered his family together.

The two large overgrown bushes, long ago strategically planted, helped conceal the entrance to the crypt. Close examination would always reveal the three steps cut into the ground that led to the small narrow door, but not every parishioner in the village knew of its existence.

"Come quickly this way." The priest pushed hard on the old wooden door and waved everyone in. It was dark and musty inside. The walls of the crypt were damp to the touch, and no one could see where they were going. Someone screamed as they caught their head on the low stone ceiling. Then suddenly, there was light. The priest had lit a candle and, from that, another one.

Everyone huddled together and waited. The large congregation now only consisted of ten or twelve people, plus the two families. The rest had scattered before the priest could shepherd them to safety. There were lots of mumblings, and someone was sobbing. He asked everyone to try and be quiet. He could see the fear in the eyes of those standing close to him.

"We will be safe here." He said reassuringly before whispering "Please, God" under his breath. The silence was unnerving, and people began holding hands, seeking comfort. Anything was better than standing alone in the semi-dark, waiting for something to happen.

Outside, the Russian tank had stopped, and an officer had opened the turret hatch and checked the area. "Our artillery has done their job well. It is of no use." He informed the rest of his crew, laughing loudly. "If there were villagers up here, they have scurried away back into their little hovels." This time the laughter came from within the tank. "Turn around, Yurchik. We need to get back to the column. There is nothing of interest here." The tank clunked and growled as it swung around, plumes of smoke bellowing from its exhaust.

Inside the crypt, they could hear nothing and do nothing. It was all about patience, waiting until perhaps someone felt brave enough to go above ground and investigate. After nearly an hour of standing in the claustrophobic crypt, Feliks had had enough. He offered to go and look, but the priest held him back. "They are less likely to kill me," he whispered, preparing to move towards the door. Feliks didn't know if he believed in that philosophy. He thought the Russians would probably shoot anyone they saw.

They all watched as the priest opened the small door, allowing the late afternoon sun to penetrate their enclosed area. He closed it quietly behind him and walked carefully around the ruined church. The place was deserted. The only sign of the tank was where it had dug into the path as it maneuvered to go back down the hill.

The priest still walked cautiously, crouching as he neared the oil drums now scattered everywhere, as the tank driver had clearly taken great delight in squashing as many as he could before leaving. Back down in the valley, he could just about see the four tanks in the distance, the last one still several metres behind, having not yet caught up with the others. He also saw the villagers making their way back up to the church. They had worked things out, and they knew the danger was over. They also knew there was a wedding to attend.

The priest hitched his white linen vestment up and ran back to the crypt. Those waiting inside held their breath when the door was suddenly flung open. Everyone seemed to exhale simultaneously as they saw the smiling priest waving them out. Some shielded their eyes from the sun, and others held their arms aloft in joy. The young couple didn't stop, and they hurried around to the front of the church and took up their positions, almost as if nothing had happened.

Yeva and Feliks stood smiling as more and more people arrived. The younger ones hurriedly ran towards them, the older villagers puffing and panting from their climb. The number seemed to have grown. There was far more now than earlier. This was an act of defiance involving the whole village.

Feliks couldn't control his emotions, and he began clapping. Yeva joined in, as did her mother and sister. Within seconds everyone standing by the altar was showing their appreciation and applauding the new arrivals.

Feliks and Yeva might not have **had** many possessions to call their own as they beg**a**n their journey as husband and wife, but they had each other and a wealth of love from everyone there. War-torn Ukraine had offered them nothing on this special day, but they were in love and, as we know, that particular emotion knows no boundaries. It doesn't stop existing just because the church you were just married in is now in ruins.

ABOUT THE AUTHOR

Peter Bissett has always been creative. He started writing very young, mainly poetry, and wrote stories for his children as they grew up. Now retired and living in Somerset, Peter is able to indulge his passion for writing and has 16 books published in paperback and on Amazon in the Kindle format, covering a wide range of genres for children and for adults, including collections of short stories. He writes "Whatever comes into my head" and so the subject matter is varied and interesting, sometimes allowing his sense of humour full rein.

OTHER BOOKS BY THE AUTHOR
THE JOURNEY BACK
CAT KISSES AND DOG BREATH
TROUSERS ROUND MY ANKLES
DRESSED FOR BED
TREASONABLE WORDS
THE SAND SPIRITS
AN EXTRA DEADLY SIN
THEIR DARKEST SECRETS
THE LIST

SHORT STORIES
GHOST STORIES 2 DIE 4
A COCKTAIL FULL OF WORDS
PASSING THIS WAY BUT ONCE

CHILDREN'S STORIES
MR. MOLE THE GREENKEEPER
JUST FOUR DOGS
MORE FOUR DOGS

Printed in Great Britain
by Amazon

14926556R00149